A Twist In The Tale

INCREDIBLE ADVENTURES

EDITED BY DAISY JOB

First published in Great Britain in 2023 by:

 Young**Writers**® ─ Est. 1991 ─

Young Writers
Remus House
Coltsfoot Drive
Peterborough
PE2 9BF
Telephone: 01733 890066
Website: www.youngwriters.co.uk

Printed and bound in the UK by BookPrintingUK
Website: www.bookprintinguk.com
YB0537N

Foreword

Welcome, Reader!

For our latest competition A Twist in the Tale, we challenged primary school students to write a story in just 100 words that will surprise the reader. They could add a twist to an existing tale, show us a new perspective or simply write an original story.

The authors in this anthology have given us some creative new perspectives on tales we thought we knew, and written stories that are sure to surprise! The result is a thrilling and absorbing collection of stories written in a variety of styles, and it's a testament to the creativity of these young authors. Be prepared for shock endings, unusual characters and amazing creativity!

Here at Young Writers it's our aim to inspire the next generation and instill in them a love of creative writing, and what better way than to see their work in print? The imagination and skill within these pages are proof that we might just be achieving that aim! Congratulations to each of these fantastic authors.

Contents

Greatfield Park Primary School, Up Hatherley

Jessica Guppy (11)	65
Willow Hicks (10)	66
James Townley (10)	67
Oli Redfearn (11)	68
Oliver Philimore (11)	69
Joshua Goodman (11)	70
Poppy Jones (11)	71
Emilia Latham (10)	72
Jessica Jenkins (11)	73
Lola Kitchen (10)	74
Esma Ayguner (11)	75
Mylo Boyle (10)	76
Daniel Wrench (11)	77
Noah Birt (11)	78
Rosie McDermott (11)	79
Mia O'Donnell (10)	80
Kian Steed (10)	81
Mia Ling (10)	82
Darcey Curran (10)	83
Autumn Cotton-Bettgridge (11)	84
Isaac Chow (10)	85

Holland Junior School, Hurst Green

Maeve Moran (7)	86
Leo Messi (10)	87
Evalyn Casey (7)	88
Jessica Dean (9)	89
Freddy Seyit (10)	90
Neve O'Neill (10)	91
Francesca Arcidiacono (9)	92
Dominic Kromalicki (10)	93
Joseph Levin (8)	94
Mia Kimber (9)	95
Archie Alexander (10)	96
Benjamin Jones (9)	97
Tommy England (7)	98
Cleo Wyatt (8)	99
Evelyn Butcher (9)	100
Taya Steptoe (8)	101
Rosie Mann (9)	102
Alex Hall (9)	103

Kaydra Darko (9)	104
Benjamin Carman (9)	105
Buddy Krol (8)	106
Louis Swindells	107
Benjamin Whitelock (9)	108
Tabitha Windett (7)	109
Freddie Funnell (10)	110
Alexis Thomas-Morris (10)	111
Emily Buckham (7)	112
Demi Oosthuizen (10)	113
Isobel Eltringham (9)	114
Tillie Sene (7)	115
Summer Smith (9)	116
Matthew Mitrovic (10)	117
Ada Kelly (10)	118
Daisy Mann (9)	119
Nell Kelly (8)	120

Mintlaw Primary School, Mintlaw

Jessica Taylor (10)	121
Reuben Price (10)	122
Michael Burke (10)	123
Demi-Rose Parry (10)	124
Alayah McLeod (10)	125
Isla Elrick (10)	126
Cooper Leslie (10)	127
Millie Hunter (10)	128
Subhan Anwar (10)	129
Indi Taylor (10)	130
Archie Henderson (10)	131
Hayden Reid (9)	132
Isla Robbie (10)	133
Cammie Chan (10)	134
Charlie Watt (9)	135
Ugne Skersyte (10)	136
Alyssia Dawson (10)	137
Joseph Macmillan (10)	138
Zoey Jamieson (10)	139
Hamish Bream (10)	140
Jacob Mayhew (10)	141
Daniel Milne (10)	142

Shifnal Primary School, Shifnal

Lily Lewis (10)	143
Isla-Rose Wootton (10)	144
Jessie Zhao	145
Ruby White (10)	146
Maggie Barnes	147
Betsy Simpson (11)	148
Aoife Boden (9)	149
Emma Heritage-Owen (10)	150
Harriet Goodchild	151
Dhron Narender-Rajan	152
Lillian Whitfield	153
Jamie Broome (9)	154
Elsie Clewes	155
Harry Hemsley (10)	156
Alfie	157
Megan Garbett	158
James Grisswell (10)	159
Ava Mason (11)	160
Miley Federico (11)	161
Grace Allatt (11)	162
Megan Aston (11)	163
Kaitlyn Rowley (9)	164

Tangmere Primary Academy, Tangmere

Oscar Cross (10)	165
Dylan Brown (11)	166
Amelia Luff (10)	167
Theo Read (11)	168
Peyton Arnold-Jackman (10)	169
Max Stringer (10)	170
Honey Clare (10)	171
Kayowa Nosiru (11)	172
Eloise Bulbeck (11)	173
Annabel Ridley (11)	174
Julia Socha (11)	175
Darcy Bagnall (10)	176
Emmie Hunt (11)	177
Margaret Stockdale (10)	178
Leo Hewitt (11)	179
Cruz Bunce (10)	180
Francessca Smith (11)	181
Jake Burley (10)	182

Emma Walker (10)	183
Frank Wright (10)	184
Tia-Louise Keenan (10)	185
Ami Pierce (10)	186
Ava Doherty (10)	187
Amelia Miksza (11)	188

The Stories

THE LITTLE GOOD RAVEN

In school, there was a girl called Raven. She was going to class when she found a book in her locker. She saw a picture of her mother as 'wanted'.
Raven said, "I've got to go and find Apple."
Apple was her best friend. As she heard Apple talking to friends, Raven's mother appeared.
"Ha! So you found out."
"Yes," said Raven.
Apple ran down to the evil mother, Regina. Regina threatened Raven to not tell anyone. Raven found out that she had magic and trapped her mother in a mirror. Apple said, "Thank you, Raven."
"Oh, it was nothing."

Sophie Boylan (8)

Blackmoor Park Junior School, Liverpool

A MYSTERY!

Once upon a time, there was a boy named Archie. Archie wakes up in the morning so he won't miss the bus. When he arrives, he goes to get something from his locker. As soon as he opens it, he teleports to a different world.
He walks around until he finds a red button on the floor saying,
'This is dangerous!'
Suddenly he sees a monster heading towards him fast. Archie grabs several rocks and throws them. The monster suddenly vanishes. Archie hesitatingly presses the button.
He travels back to his world, but he knows something is wrong. It's changed!

Archchagan Kirubakaran (8)

Blackmoor Park Junior School, Liverpool

THE TWISTER

It was an epic battle. CrystalGirl and DogBoy were fighting evil. They got away and stumbled upon an entrance. They went through it. They hid in a box. After the queen came by they got out and ran as fast as they could. They ran into the closest room and found the queen's money room. The queen found them and threw the kids in her basement. "We're trapped!" said CrystalGirl.

"Look, a tunnel!"

They crawled through into a strange room with strange people on a big screen. They saw themselves and realised they were actually a TV show.

Hali Houghton (8)

Blackmoor Park Junior School, Liverpool

THE DELICIOUS, SHINY, PINK SHOE

Molly, her mum and her sister went shopping for shoes. They went into the shoe shop and carefully looked at which shoe they were going to pick for Molly. Something suddenly caught Molly's eye. She wanted to try them on but they looked very odd. Molly put her foot into the shiny, pink shoe and bells rang!

A person appeared and said the shoe was actually a shiny, pink cake.

Molly won the 'cake shoe' competition and was awarded a year's worth of free cake. Molly tasted the shiny, pink cake, it was delicious. Molly called it the delicious cake!

Mya Hughes (8)

Blackmoor Park Junior School, Liverpool

SHE BEAST

As the beast changed back into a prince, Belle started to feel a bit odd. Once the beast had changed back completely, he noticed that Belle had fainted. He darted over to Mrs Pots who'd got her a pillow and a hot cloth for her head.

Then, at that very moment, an elderly lady burst through the doors.

"This is your final test," she whispered softly, and then was off once more.

He searched high and low for the woman but he could not find her. She was gone... But by then, Belle was 100% beast!

"I love you anyway."

Annabelle Doyle (10)

Blackmoor Park Junior School, Liverpool

PLANET-X

Danny and Mia had a normal life until they started to suspect their mum had been replaced by a robot! Their dad worked at NASA and had alien technology, and also a spaceship. They used this to get away from their mum.

They stole the ship and tech and flew into space. They had to get to Planet-X as soon as possible. They couldn't find it until they got into a portal. There it was, Planet-X, right in front of them. When they landed they were surrounded by evil robot mums! But they had the tech. They pressed a button...

Mia Houghton (10)

Blackmoor Park Junior School, Liverpool

WHEN I WAS LITTLE

When I was little, I used to knock on trees and see if a fairy would open a magical door and invite me in for a tea party. One day, I was taking a soothing stroll in the forest. The brown, autumnal leaves crunched under my feet. The trees calmly danced in the soft breeze. It was a picturesque day. Since I was in the forest, I started knocking on the trees. I knocked on this peculiar-looking tree, and to my surprise, a fairy opened an enchanting, pink door! She invited me inside and ended up cooking and eating me...

India Farmer (10)
Blackmoor Park Junior School, Liverpool

THE ANIMAL DREAM

Once upon a time, a boy called Jay was living a normal life, but one day his mum didn't pick him up. He decided to walk home by himself, but he got lost in the woods and he started to hear animals, and then he went to discover and then the animal started speaking and then he could actually understand them, so he was so happy. He thought it was strange but pretty cool and fun, so every animal he approached he had a conversation with them, but it turned out it was a dream after all.

Rosie Burke (9)

Blackmoor Park Junior School, Liverpool

THE UNKNOWN MURDERER

Once there was a girl named Aisha. She was out with her friends but there was meant to be an unknown killer, but the girls didn't believe it so they still stayed. Soon, Aisha and her friend Shera were looking for Bethany, Shera's twin. Long story short, they couldn't find her.

Aisha soon went to sleep. Shera cried her heart out.

When Aisha woke up she couldn't find Shera at all. That day, she went home and she woke up. That was a relief, but then again, it wasn't... Soon she went missing and her friends, well, they're gone.

Rebecca Quigley (9)
Carbrain Primary School, Cumbernauld

CHRISTMAS IS RUINED

Once upon a time at the North Pole, Santa was very jolly, but not for long... He asked an elf for warm milk, but he was evil! He went to the kitchen and put poison in Santa's drink and gave it to him. Santa went crazy! He went and ate all the elves and he went to his sleigh and rode it to the villain. He teamed up with 'The Grinch' to ruin Christmas! They stole Christmas trees.

Then Cindy Loo came out. She said, "What about Christmas?"

Santa had a vision. Then he said, "Oh no! Christmas, it's gone!"

Billie Ann Hill (10)

Carbrain Primary School, Cumbernauld

THE ENDLESS SHOP

One day, Billy and John were shopping and they could not find a place to buy things, everything was repeating! They were exploring and John found a really tall ladder. John was saying to climb it, but Billy was saying not to climb it because it was too dangerous. John convinced Billy to climb the ladder.

When climbing the ladder, Billy fell off! Then John caught Billy with one hand, and someone smacked John's hand off the ladder.

Billy woke up in a bed and John was not real and Billy saw the exit and he escaped.

Oliver Markowski (9)
Carbrain Primary School, Cumbernauld

THE MYSTERY OF THE WHIRLPOOL

Once upon a time, there were three girls called Leah, Sarah and Katie and they were at the beach. All of them were playing and they did not notice the whirlpool open. Leah said, "Let's go into the sea," and they went in.
They sank but they could breathe. They had scales. They were mermaids! They had so much fun. When it was nighttime it was scary! Sharks and squids were everywhere! Leah had a panic attack. Sarah and Katie calmed her down. What was going to happen to them? Bad stuff was happening.

Gunjan Sharma (10)
Carbrain Primary School, Cumbernauld

THE DANGEROUS DAY

One day, in 1998, two girls were visiting their uncle, the Prime Minister, who had a big castle. They walked around it and got to see everything.
Then an hour later, Lilly went into another room. She bumped into the Prime Minister. He grabbed her! Maggie went into the room her sister was in. She saw her sister Lilly. She had turned into a green, big monster! Maggie tried to make her sister human again, but it made it worse. She tried and tried and tried but it never worked! Maggie said she had the worst day ever.

Darianny De Leon Cuevas (10)
Carbrain Primary School, Cumbernauld

THE BOY WHO LOST HIS FRIEND

One day, there were two boys that went to their friend's house to play some video games, but one of their friends had been teleported to a world that had existed for a thousand years and nobody knew about it. If Bruce's friends didn't make it in time, Toni would die. If not, they would be separated from each other for eternity.

Then Bruce got angry and something was glowing inside his body! Bruce had superpowers. He was flying to go and find his friend. Bruce carried his friend to his house.

Nathan Obezuwa Alexander (9)
Carbrain Primary School, Cumbernauld

THE PORTAL TREE

Messi is walking in the jungle and Ronaldo comes out of a weird portal tree. They go inside and it takes them to a football pitch, and Ronaldo scores a screamer from the halfway line, then he gets stuck in a weird hole. Messi helps him out.
The portal closes. They try to run and try to make it but they do not make it. They try to get it back and they can't, but also the pitch is right beside the jungle. They escape through the doors and they get back to the jungle, Messi and Cristiano Ronaldo.

Kai Welsh (9)
Carbrain Primary School, Cumbernauld

THE DREAM DREAMERS

It all started in a dark, abandoned park. The two girls found it in the middle of nowhere, but then Lily and Layla saw a black hole appear and it sucked both of them in!

They saw a world no one else had seen. They saw a red sky, black clouds and so on. They wandered about for some minutes and finally found something; a house! But then it started moving and then the house ran away.

Then they saw a secret exit, it was so far and they ran. Suddenly as they pushed the door they both woke up.

Daniella Dada (9)

Carbrain Primary School, Cumbernauld

SLIME FACTORY

I went to my mum's room to play Slime Rancher. I started to play it and the TV pulled me into the game!

The music went on and I found a baby slime and I kept it as a pet and started to get more slimes. The first slime is the pink slime, then the tabby slime and rock slime. Then I made homes for them to get the stuff they need. A tar formed and I had to throw it in the slime ocean.

I felt something, then a portal formed but I fell asleep.

Alex Findlay (8)

Carbrain Primary School, Cumbernauld

STUCK AS A CHUBBY CHICK

One time, me and a group of my friends went to school. When we went to school we did maths and I had to go to the toilet.

There was a portal and when I went into the portal, I got sucked into a video game. The video game was called The Chubby Chick and I became a chubby chick, and I got a bit weird because there was a black spot so I went over to the black spot and it was a monster. *Ahhh!* So I tried to run but it ran after me.

Cooper Wildridge (8)
Carbrain Primary School, Cumbernauld

THE STRANGE FOOTBALL PITCH

CR7 went to the football pitch. He did some training. Next, he played a game. His team won 9-5.

Strange things started to happen. Water made a mess on the table. The floodlights started to flicker and the window smashed. Someone got hurt with a football.

Next, CR7 played his PS5. The PS5 got too hot and it exploded. CR7 jumped out of the window, saved his manager and got paid a lot of money.

Cody Robertson (8)

Carbrain Primary School, Cumbernauld

TREASURE AT THE BEACH

One time, a dog and cat went to a beach and they were starting to dig up the beach. They were hunting for treasure. They found a chest, but there was a lock.

They began to dig for the key. They found the key and unlocked the treasure chest. The cat and dog went to a shop to get some treats. Every day they were happy and the best of friends.

Lexi-Rose Johnston (9)

Carbrain Primary School, Cumbernauld

UNSPEAKABLE

Late one evening in the middle of the forest, the boy and the wolf met. The boy called Unspeakable screamed then ran away then came back to fight the werewolf. The werewolf bit Unspeakable and he then turned into a werewolf too. They became friends and lived happily ever after.

Rhonan McMahon (9)
Carbrain Primary School, Cumbernauld

THE EXTREMELY BORING SUMMER CAMP

"Mum! I'm late for school!"

"No! You're not going, you're going where you belong. You're going to summer camp!"

"What!? I can't believe I'm doing this. This is boring! All they do is work and read, it's so boring!"

At lunch the line is so long, I can't think what to eat.

"Don't say anything to the lunch lady!"

"What? Ashley! Maisy! What're you doing here?"

"I'm here because I hit my mum."

"Why!?"

"She hates me, so I did that."

"Well, I'm here because I pushed her down the stairs."

"God! Maisy, I didn't know you were violent."

Rafael Saint McCurdy (9)
Christ Church CE Primary School, Lichfield

TO APE OR NOT TO APE

One day, Alph Brittany and Charlie were flying. They were excited to be going back home but then...

"Argh," screamed Alph.

Suddenly, they were going down... They crashed and looked around. They could see an Arctic ape on the distant tundra. He started charging towards them. Quickly, they ran for their lives but he grabbed them and started waving them around. As he waved they flew out of his beastly hand and into the air heading towards the poisonous forest. Luckily, the sky parted and they landed inside their spaceship.

"Did that really happen?" asked Charlie.

"Did what?" replied Alph.

Nathaniel Swallow (8)

Christ Church CE Primary School, Lichfield

THE WRECKED PRINCIPAL

One stormy day, this innocent little girl called Sienna was at school studying for a test. Twenty minutes later, while in class, the principal was her new maths teacher, but she didn't mind! It was when he spoke that she changed her mind. Suddenly, the windows broke and his eyes turned emerald green!

Everyone huddled together in horror... all except Sienna. Quickly, her eyes turned diamond blue! The war had only just begun... Sienna leapt into the air, finding herself hovering! She felt energy build up inside her soul and then, without warning, she launched down to mark... the *start*!?

D H (9)

Christ Church CE Primary School, Lichfield

WITCH AND BOB NIGEL

One day there was a little girl called Witch and she had just appeared in a magical land with her brother, Bob Nigel. They found a sweet gingerbread house. They were evaporating the sugar. Then Hansel caught them and put their cauldron on the boiling fire.

"Make yourselves at home," said Hansel.

"W-w-what?" said Bob. "I thought you were going to eat me!"

Gretel said, "Eww, I hate the taste of children!"

Suddenly, Gretel and Hansel went to the human world instead of Bob and Witch and lived as Hansel and Gretel, who lived the normal story life.

Daisy Yates (8)

Christ Church CE Primary School, Lichfield

THE WEREWOLVES/LSC GIRLS

Once upon a time, there lived fourteen girls. Their names were Lulu, Leah, Lucy, Laya, Lynn, Lily, Lenna, Liah, Lexi, Lyla, Leli, Laila, Lavender, Lenie and Lacey. On this day, they made their way to the school, Lavender High School.

"Leah, are you excited for our cinema day?" Lili asked noisily.

The fourteen girls arrived at the cinema and they got VIP tickets.

Next, only one survived. The other thirteen turned into... werewolves! How could Lulu save them from being killed by zombies!?

The next day, Lulu woke up from a terrible dream. She saw that they were dead!

Imogen Wheatley (8)
Christ Church CE Primary School, Lichfield

THE SELFISH RAPUNZEL

Once upon a time, there lived a selfish teenager, Rapunzel, and a sweet-hearted Mother Gothel. One day, Rapunzel discovered that her hair was getting shorter and her nails were getting longer by the second. You see, Mother Gothel was really nice and Rapunzel was the meanest person in the universe.

Gothel explained that Rapunzel should go get some plants to break the curse. But guess what? The selfish brat just screamed no, right in the poor woman's face.

Soon enough, Mother Gothel agreed that she would go and get the plants for her beloved daughter. But did she deserve it?

Emilia Rowland (8)
Christ Church CE Primary School, Lichfield

THE MYSTERY GIRL WHO MAKES PEOPLE DISAPPEAR

On Tuesday, a new girl came to my school, but the two people who sat next to her disappeared. We all went to look for them. When we came back, everyone except her on the table was gone. We all looked at each other.

A couple of days later we went on a school trip. Everyone on the coach had disappeared. It was only me, Olive, Mr Hikes and Grace, the sus one.
"Right, Grace," said Mr Hikes, "are you the one who made everyone d-disappear?" Mr Hikes sounded scared.
"Yes?"
"Where is everyone then?"
"On Planet Mars!"

Rose Hardy (8)
Christ Church CE Primary School, Lichfield

THE END OF THE WORLD

One normal day, Evelyne and Quint sat next to each other on the school bus. Suddenly, both sides of the bus shuddered. Evelyne looked up out of the window and saw a giant X portal, with massive monsters coming out, but the bus went and drove into the playground.

The worst thing happened. Everyone apart from Quint and Evelyne turned into Among Us characters. All of the teachers turned into zombies. So Evelyne took Quint to the treehouse to start to live there, where they found a deer fox. "But that's meant to be super legendary!" said Quint, surprised.

Elsa Cantliff (8)
Christ Church CE Primary School, Lichfield

EDGAR'S SPOOKY ADVENTURE

Once upon a shriek, there lived a cool, unexpected boy called Edgar who was mad about monsters and knew next door was haunted. Everyone else had proof so he wondered if he could make it a hit on his webshow.

He went inside and heard lots of eerie noises. He crept upstairs and glared around the room. Nothing but beds. So he looked in the bathroom. Nothing. Kitchen? Nothing. Garden? Nothing. Nothing! Nothing!

Sadly, Edgar walked home with no proof that the house was haunted. Edgar felt disappointed, but left with a knowing smile never giving up on his search.

Inayaah Ahmad (9)
Christ Church CE Primary School, Lichfield

THE AMAZING SOMETHING THAT HAPPENED

One day, me and my sister were playing Animal Crossing when suddenly something strange happened. I was in Animal Crossing with my sister. It was amazing.

My sister dragged me everywhere because we lived on the same island. Then I said, "Hang on a second! We are in a game, but the game is Animal Crossing and it is fabulous!"

I showed my sister that I had a mermaid house. She was amazed because she loves mermaids and beaches.

Suddenly, we were back home, playing Animal Crossing together. It felt like a dream, but my sister said it was real.

Zara Atthueis-Grundy (9)
Christ Church CE Primary School, Lichfield

THE CRAZY CHRISTMAS

One Christmas Eve, everything was so peaceful until... Santa went missing! Everyone panicked like crazy. Santa's reindeer found out, so they collected girls named Zara, Merryn and Sophie.

They went around the world and after three hours, they finally found Santa in Egypt, doing the conga. It was crazy.

They reminded him about his job and he rushed straight to work. Before that, he gave them a sleigh ride home as a thank you.

The next day, they celebrated saving Christmas forever. Now, on the 24th of December, there is a feast in their village.

Sophie Scott (9)
Christ Church CE Primary School, Lichfield

AN UNKNOWN MONSTER MYSTERY

Once, a pretty girl who was 8 was doing Tudor history. Her name was Marco. Marco did not like history so when it was done, Marco was relieved. Later, she was walking to her darling home when... *Boom!*

A monster appeared! It was bright and colourful, but scary. It scared the poor girl. She ran to the nearest shelter and slammed the wooden door shut. She was petrified! Marco grabbed a long metal pole and hit the monster with it. Marco heard a groan and said sorry. It was surprisingly her best friend, Patrick. To say sorry they watched Tarzan!

Órla Browne (8)

Christ Church CE Primary School, Lichfield

CHRISTMAS LAND

Scar was putting up her Christmas tree when her parents came in. They said, "Take that down!" Then she flew up and landed in Christmas Land and figured out that she liked Christmas more than Halloween. She was a skeleton and when she met other kids they ran away and she was heartbroken, so she met Santa and helped. But she realised there was a skeleton kidnapper and she fell down a secret entrance. She felt her heart break and went back to a hidden shelter in Christmas Land. She turned into an elf and helped Santa and the reindeer.

Holly Taylor (8)

Christ Church CE Primary School, Lichfield

THE MYSTERIOUS PRIME MINISTER

One day, a 10-year-old boy called Jack wanted to know how old the Prime Minister was. That afternoon he invited his friend, Finn, over to his house to research the Prime Minister's age and it came up that the Prime Minister's age was 4. They were shocked. They couldn't believe what they had seen.

The next day, Jack rushed to school to tell people that the Prime Minister was a child. When he got to school, he insistently told Snotball, who was a massive bully, but he didn't believe him. Snotball searched it up and Jack was right.

Amelia Brett (8)
Christ Church CE Primary School, Lichfield

JACK'S INVESTIGATION

One day a boy called Jack was investigating at his school. He saw his science teacher in a secret lab making potions. Jack kept on watching him make the potions until the potions turned into something.

He was there for an hour but he couldn't believe his eyes! There were animals, Jack had never seen animals like that before. They looked like werewolves and zombies. He said to himself, "With these animals I can take over the whole city!"

As soon as he said that, he ran away and he called the police but there was no one there!

Freddie Gardner (8)

Christ Church CE Primary School, Lichfield

THE GIRL AND THE WOLF

Once there was a girl picking mushrooms and berries. One day, she brought her younger sister along but found the berries had been picked. Holly went further. Her sister got lost. She didn't know. Holly called her sis, no answer.

Then she saw the home of Shiba and she said that she'd lost her sister. Shiba whistled and a grey wolf came running. The wolf took them to her. The girl screamed. The wolf growled. Holly thought Shiba was a witch, but the wolf picked her up and took her home. They found mushrooms and the basket next to her.

Jessica Long (8)
Christ Church CE Primary School, Lichfield

IN THE DEAD OF NIGHT

In a kingdom, far in the north, the royal family needed their daughter called Snowflake to be the ruler of the kingdom. Well, Snowflake didn't want to rule but her younger sister, Ruby, did. Ruby was an obedient, smart girl and was sure to be a perfect ruler. One of the things the ruler had to do was keep the Northern Lights from shattering. The next day, it was decided Snowflake would be ruler, but was this a good idea? In the dead of night, there was a rumbling, a cracking. The Northern Lights was shattering. The kingdom had fallen!

Merryn Sharkey (8)
Christ Church CE Primary School, Lichfield

MILLY'S BASEMENT

One day, Milly asked her mum what was in the basement. Her mum said not to go in because she'd heard a noise in there. When her mum dropped her at school, she investigated with her friends, Grace and Jimmy. They said her mum was right!

That afternoon she crept down the stairs to the basement. She took a deep breath. You wouldn't believe what she saw. Stood there was a tall, colourful clown! Although this was not what she was expecting, she gazed across the room in disbelief. There was an area with food, she wanted to explore more.

Siaane Shoker (9)

Christ Church CE Primary School, Lichfield

THE GIRL WITH UNKNOWN POWERS

Once upon a time, a little girl called Felicity thought she was ordinary, but one day at school it all changed. She was in class at lunch when she saw a wall. Her eyesight started going colourful and she could see through the wall. She fell over in shock, but her body didn't touch the ground. She was surprisingly rising upwards. She was flying. She flew and flew but started to fall down and down and realised she had turned into a dog! She landed on a trampoline and she was herself again. She found she couldn't control her powers!

Isabelle Bailey (9)
Christ Church CE Primary School, Lichfield

ONE COLD FROSTY WINTER'S DAY

Once upon a time, there was a little girl called Mila. She lived in Coldland. Because of this, she always wrapped up warm in her fluffy pom-pom hat and sparkly mittens.

One day she was walking and she tripped over a rusty old key. She picked it up and, *whoosh*, she was zooming through the air and, *pop!* She was in a land filled with sweets and chocolate. It was heaven. Lakes filled with chocolate and mountains of candy canes and sugar plums.

But it was too good to be true, and it was. It was all an amazing dream.

Aurelia Santomassimo (9)
Christ Church CE Primary School, Lichfield

THE UNEXPECTED NEIGHBOUR

Once there was a little girl called Christie and her neighbour was moving out. She was really upset that the old lady was moving out, but life is life. Christie helped the old lady pack her bags to say her last goodbye.

The next day, whilst Christie was getting changed, she heard a noise. There was a man and he was moving into the house next to Christie. Christie didn't like the way he looked. When he was out, Christie went inside his house and searched. You won't believe it, he was a villain! Christie caught him red-handed.

Libby Clayton (9)
Christ Church CE Primary School, Lichfield

SPACE BAND ON MARS

George Rocket jumped out of his seat when the science teacher went out of the classroom. This was a science lesson, so he knew what song to play. As George and his band played the longest song ever, a purple, swirly portal opened and sucked the Earthlings (George, Nelia and Bash) inside.

They looked around at red rocks, a red sky and huge craters.

"We're on Mars!"

They had to escape. They found some balloons and a metal box. George had a fan in his bag for some reason, so he made a ship to blast into space.

Oliver Kayran (8)
Christ Church CE Primary School, Lichfield

THE DAY IT ALL CHANGED

One day, me and Penny were walking to school when I saw the light flicker. We left it, but when we got to school, everyone else had gone!
We looked in the classroom. It looked like a plan was about to happen, everything was so perfect. But the room had a bad feeling. On Ella's table was a Post-it note that said 'the hall'. So we ran to the hall, but sadly they'd moved on.
We saw another Post-it note, it said 'Year 6 classroom', so we ran to the classroom but no one was there. What would happen next...?

Evelyne Hollinsworth (8)
Christ Church CE Primary School, Lichfield

THE JOURNEY TO THE CENTRE OF THE WORLD

Hello, I've got an old story to tell you about a true myth.

Once upon a time, a girl named Megan believed that at the core of the world lived phoenixes, but most people didn't believe her. One day, she decided she'd dig to the core of the world, and so she did. Surprisingly, she was right, and some beautiful, splendid types of phoenix came and landed on her shoulder.

Suddenly, Megan awoke to the sound of her mum calling her for breakfast. It must have been a dream! She looked down to see a burn. Was it a dream?

Emma Ballantyne (9)

Christ Church CE Primary School, Lichfield

THE GIRL WHO MAY OR MAY NOT HAVE BEEN SLAIN BY A WOLF

Once upon a time, not long ago, a young girl called Mindy was ambling to her Grandad's, but suddenly a wolf appeared, but she wasn't scared or petrified. She said hi and patted it on the head gently, but the wolf didn't like that. He sharply stood and ran for her. Mindy got shocked and at just the minute he pounced, she found herself awakening, but she wasn't in her bedroom. She was in the middle of the forest in the spot she was about to get pounced on.
Was it a dream or reality? Who knows, maybe the wolf...?

Florence Fryer (8)
Christ Church CE Primary School, Lichfield

UNEXPECTED SANTA

One snowy day a small, cute deer fox trundled in the deep snow. The deer fox was lost and didn't have a home. Suddenly, Twig (the deer fox) saw a light, it was Santa's grotto. Santa stepped out of the door and he said, "Oh, hello, Twig."
Santa took Twig inside for a cookie and warm milk. When Santa took his hat off, Twig noticed that... Santa was a gingerbread man! Twig was shocked and went to tell Mrs Claus, but she was asleep and the gingerbread Santa told Twig that it was okay and to not be afraid.

Ella Thurlby (8)
Christ Church CE Primary School, Lichfield

DAN AND THE CURSED FOREST OF HORROR

In a cursed forest Dan stood, terrified. He called the town hero, but no one came to his rescue. Suddenly, a bolt of lightning hit him. After that, Dan realised that he could shoot lightning out of his hands and eyes. He could also shape-shift. Later on, he was having fun back at home, but then the town superhero tried to strangle him. Now it was like he was the town's supervillain! Just then, he teleported to a cliff. Dan struck him with a huge lightning bolt, then he teleported back and grabbed him in a headlock.

Jacob McGrath (8)

Christ Church CE Primary School, Lichfield

MY NEW NEIGHBOUR

Today I woke up and I found out my neighbour was coming today! I got ready and enjoyed my cornflakes. I was about to go out and meet my new neighbour when a letter came through the door. I read the letter and it told me to look through the window.

Right then I looked through the window at a white figure with a business suit. He pulled up a sign saying: 'Turn around'. Lights flickered as I turned around. There he was, my neighbour standing behind me. This time I saw his tentacles and he was holding a knife...

Megan Cooke (9)
Christ Church CE Primary School, Lichfield

A MYSTERIOUS DAY AT SCHOOL

Once upon a time, I arrived at school thinking it was an ordinary day, but what it turned out to be was not ordinary. First, there was nobody to greet me, but I took no notice of that. I couldn't find a teacher anywhere when I got inside. My jaw dropped as I darted anxiously through the huge school. There were no teachers! Why?
I was about to run towards the door when I realised that all the kids had left. As I sprinted hurriedly towards the nearest exit, I tripped and went flying into the door. I was out...

Grace C (9)

Christ Church CE Primary School, Lichfield

THE MAGICAL CANDY HOUSE

One day it was a normal, boring school lesson, but Finn had an idea because it was raining. Finn had a plan. At lunch, he would leave school and go into a forest to find a massive candy house.

Finn went to go and check it out. He went and inside it was full of chocolate. Finn got stuck in there and a candy monster was chasing him around until he started hiding, but Finn didn't know the candy monster could smell him.

Then Finn found a secret exit to get out of the house and he managed to escape.

Finn Maguire-Turner (8)
Christ Church CE Primary School, Lichfield

A LITTLE BOY'S DREAM

It was a beautiful sunny morning, and one little boy wanted to go on an adventure. So he packed his bags and went. He saw a wondrous wood of trees, it was beautiful. Then he climbed hills. After that, he climbed up cliffs.

Suddenly, he got to the top of the cliffs and he saw a castle. He would have to sneak inside. He thought of a plan, then he saw the gate open. After that, he saw the guards and they fought. He knocked the guards out and went home.

Then he found out it was all a dream.

Alfie Jones (9)
Christ Church CE Primary School, Lichfield

MY CRAZY NEIGHBOUR

One sunny day, when I moved to California, I went out to look around and I asked my neighbour to dog-sit my dog. I went to see the Golden Gate Bridge but when I got back from the bridge, my precious dog had disappeared and my neighbour had scars all over her arm.

I asked my neighbour what had happened, and she replied that she didn't know. I asked if she was sure, and she said yes. She asked me to come inside to take a look and just as I was about to agree with her, she killed me...

Freddie Smyth (8)
Christ Church CE Primary School, Lichfield

WEIRD TRIP

George is a normal boy. Today he went on a school trip. When they were on the way to the place, the bus broke down and they went out. It was boiling hot so they went into the cave. It was really dark so they went to get a torch then all went back in. When they went back in, they saw a giant rat! They all screamed. They all ran out. Then George said, "I think that we woke it up!"
Then a stomping sound came out of the cave. It was the rat. Then a phoenix ate it.

Felix He (8)
Christ Church CE Primary School, Lichfield

THE NORTHERN LIGHTS

The Northern Lights cracked into 100 pieces and came raining down on me, the rabbit and the fox. You probably haven't heard of me, because I am very rare. My mum and dad's star is the brightest glowing star ever in history. My mum told me I had a magical mind, but the star was fading and so was my memory. I can hear them whispering in the darkness of the woods. Also, my friend Twig helps me fight it. She is a black fox and a big part of my life and my heart.

Penelope Cooke (9)
Christ Church CE Primary School, Lichfield

REUNITED

On a misty, dark night, a pair of twins got separated. One very special twin, called Leo, went to a lovely, kind lady called Leorna. The other twin, called Lola, went to a sweet, caring man called Lincoln.

10 years passed and they both went to the same school. As the day went by, a creepy, dangerous robber had broken out of jail. Suddenly, that robber kidnapped the twins. They had been killed. They had both gone home, but their parents could still see them...

Ettie Worth (9)

Christ Church CE Primary School, Lichfield

THE BAD GORILLA

Once there was a gorilla. His dad was a robber and they lived in a garage but Johnny always pretended to do it because he did not want to do it. He just wanted to be normal. He normally was the getaway driver, so he went to the drop-off to grab something and he did it quickly so they did not suspect anything. One time he got caught in a traffic jam, so his dad went from the place they robbed. They got arrested and he had a talk and tried to lie to his dad.

Tommy Foulsham (8)
Christ Church CE Primary School, Lichfield

SOMETHING BAD HAPPENED AT SCHOOL

It was just a normal day at school doing maths, but when I put my pencil down it rolled off the table. My book did the same. So I went to pick them up but something hit my head. It was the rubber. Then the table fell, then the whole classroom! So I ran, but I got knocked out and woke up in a helicopter.

It turned out a huge monster had pushed the school over. At least we were safe for now, but we thought it would come back even stronger than before.

William Cotter-Speake (9)

Christ Church CE Primary School, Lichfield

THE PRIME MINISTER BOY

One night a little boy was asleep and he had a very good dream that he was the president. He couldn't believe it, and he was woken up by his dog licking him.

He went back to sleep and he woke up to get ready for school, but he woke up in a mansion. He put on his clothes, he opened the door and he went outside to a fancy car. He went to the Prime Minister's place and he found out that he was the Prime Minister and he was in charge.

Lucas Meeson (9)
Christ Church CE Primary School, Lichfield

THE TWIST OF THE WOLF

Once upon a time, there was a Big Bad Riding Hood and a Little Grey Wolf. Little Grey Wolf went to visit old Grandma Wolf so Little Grey Wolf could deliver pork chops to her. But as he went on, Big Bad Riding Hood spotted him.

Finally, Little Grey Wolf arrived at Grandma's, then he ate her and pretended to be her. After, Big Bad Riding Hood arrived and Little Grey Wolf ate Big Bad Riding Hood.

William James (8)

Christ Church CE Primary School, Lichfield

THE THREE LITTLE WOLVES

There were once three little wolves who lived in a three-storey house. One lived on the first storey, one lived on the second and one lived on the third. One day, a big pig came into the house and ate the first wolf. Then the pig went up the stairs and ate the second wolf. Then the pig went up the stairs but it didn't eat the wolf, the wolf ate the pig. And they all lived unhappily ever after.

William Gransden (9)
Christ Church CE Primary School, Lichfield

GEORGIE'S SCHOOL TRIP WENT WRONG

In the morning, Georgie went on a school trip. The coach said to her that he went the wrong way! He wasn't looking and then, *crash!*
Georgie was in luck that she wasn't hurt. But then she saw Wednesday Addams. Wednesday was actually Georgie's friend. Georgie was welcomed to Wednesday's house. Wednesday's mum was not happy that Georgie was in her house.

Poppy Bailey (8)
Christ Church CE Primary School, Lichfield

THE MYSTICAL FIELD

On one sunny day, in a calming field, I was stretching my wings and flying. I got a bit tired so I sat down on the dry floor. So did my axolotl friend. As we were lying down, a corn jumped out of its stem and jumped around me like it wanted to be my friend. So I pat it on its head and I said that it could be my jolly friend. We all hopped away to the tall pastel castle.

Olivia Stuller (8)
Christ Church CE Primary School, Lichfield

THE BIG PIG

One day there was a big pig. One day the big pig looked out of his window and saw three little wolves and they were trying to blow the house down. They eventually did it, but when they got in all they wanted was to say hi!

Joshua Holloway (9)
Christ Church CE Primary School, Lichfield

STORM

Midnight was approaching along with a horrendous storm. The glimmering, glistening stars were enveloped in a murky overcoat of cloud. Storm was sitting peacefully on her windowsill, examining the sudden luminous shots of lightning. Her hair was as black as a raven's plumage. Deep vivid indigo eyes and hazel freckles embellished her face. She loved lightning!

Her best friend arrived. As she removed her shoes, Storm noticed an official-looking 'Villain Society' membership card, bearing her friend's name. "What is this!?" she exclaimed.

Suddenly, a strange, dark shadow appeared, her friend vanished and a jagged sword appeared at Storm's feet!

Jessica Guppy (11)
Greatfield Park Primary School, Up Hatherley

THE BEAR

It was show-and-tell day at school, and Eugene decided to bring his pet bear - Bear. As they were walking down the corridor, Bear started growling. "Not yet," Eugene whispered.

When it was his turn to show Bear, he demanded, "Any last words?"

The class stiffened. Eugene clicked the 'big red button' and Bear leapt onto the desk and everyone started screaming. Bear ate them all alive.

"Bear! You left some blood."

Bear turned and growled.

"H-hey there, buddy..."

Then everything went black. Bear is now the ruler of the world. You must obey him. He will find you soon!

Willow Hicks (10)
Greatfield Park Primary School, Up Hatherley

WALLY AND FRED

Wally the superhero woke up in his house and went downstairs to wake Fred up. Fred was his sidekick who he found in the pet shop. Fred was a criminal's sidekick until the criminal didn't want him anymore.

Wally and Fred made breakfast until they were interrupted. This was Wally's first-ever mission. They went to the city where the criminals were robbing everything. Fred turned on him and drank a drink that made him 10 times bigger. He started destroying everything in the city. He was destroying the shops, the cafés, houses and buildings, everything, until there wasn't anything left.

James Townley (10)
Greatfield Park Primary School, Up Hatherley

THE BACK ROOMS

As Kane was finishing recording a new film, he suddenly noclipped into a mystifying place with endless hallways; seemingly infinite buzzing florescent lights and the smell of the moist carpet drove him crazy. He wandered aimlessly until he heard an unsettling noise from around the corner. He was tempted to run but was intrigued.

As Kane came around the corner he saw a black figure with long arms peering over. All of a sudden it leapt and Kane stumbled backwards. The thing picked him up and tore his limbs off, eventually snapping his neck, killing him instantly. Never seen again...

Oli Redfearn (11)

Greatfield Park Primary School, Up Hatherley

BOB'S PRIME

Once upon a time, there was a young gentleman called Bob. One Saturday, at about 10pm, he examined the kitchen fridge carefully to see if he had Prime (the energy drink). But unfortunately, he didn't, so he went to the local corner shop to get some. He goofily Griddied (danced) along the way. When he arrived he started singing, "Blue, blue Prime, green, green Prime."

Bob went to get it quickly and was full of excitement. When he saw it had all been taken by some dodgy chap! Bob then transformed into an attack helicopter and bombed the whole Earth.

Oliver Philimore (11)

Greatfield Park Primary School, Up Hatherley

THE IMPOSSIBLE MAZE

"Roll up, roll up, come in the impossible maze!" stated the old lady.

I stepped forward and exclaimed, "I will! It'll be quite fun!"

I gave her the money and plodded on in. I felt a huge gush of wind. As I looked up there were helicopters rescuing stranded people who couldn't get out of the maze! I turned around and ventured on into the maze. I checked everywhere for the exit.

Six hours passed. Suddenly I saw something glinting in the distance. It looked like a door handle! It was a secret exit. I had escaped... Or had I?

Joshua Goodman (11)
Greatfield Park Primary School, Up Hatherley

THE SPECIAL BOOK

Ella is a girl with golden hair. She has a cat called Bob and an aunt, Pheiona. They lived in a little house in Scotland.

Ella had a book very special to her. Then one day, she got up for school and her miserable aunt snarled, "Morning, rat!"

Ella said nothing and walked past. She went to get her book but it wasn't there.

"Where's my book?" questioned Ella, but Aunt Pheiona didn't answer.

Ella went to the forest and her book was in a hole, as well as her Aunt Pheiona. She was dead. Ella lived happily ever after.

Poppy Jones (11)
Greatfield Park Primary School, Up Hatherley

NEVER TO BE SEEN AGAIN!

"Miley!" Mum called out. "Don't forget to go to the woods to get some berries."
I won't forget, I thought as I sprinted to meet my friend Jack at the park.
He was fun but he was acting differently.
I realised I needed to pick those berries. I said goodbye but he grabbed my arm. I pushed him and dashed to the woods. Then I heard something and I couldn't see. I felt a cold hand on me and from that moment, Miley was never to be seen again. I really don't know what happened when my eyes were shut.

Emilia Latham (10)
Greatfield Park Primary School, Up Hatherley

A CHRISTMAS TALE

Once upon a time, there was a little girl called Snowflake. She lived in the North Pole. Snowflake had never met her parents. She was blessed with magic powers. She walked her dog and she sang. Snowflake was decorating her beautiful house. She was sweet, joyful, loving and didn't only care about herself.

The dawn broke, she woke up and found a portal in her room! She slowly walked beyond the indigo-coloured portal and she met Mr Clause and Mrs Clause.

"Wow," she gasped.

"We are your parents. We have missed you."

Jessica Jenkins (11)
Greatfield Park Primary School, Up Hatherley

MY SISTER, BETHANY

One day, Bethany got sent to boarding school because she was not very well-behaved in her old school. In her old school, she put piranhas in the swimming pool.

Ten years later, she was still at boarding school. The principal came out and joyfully said, "I am happy for you to be here."

The principal told her not to go into the forest. But she was curious. She was determined to visit the forest. In the evening she crept out of the boarding school, and to her surprise, her parents were waiting there. They were overjoyed to see her.

Lola Kitchen (10)
Greatfield Park Primary School, Up Hatherley

SUMMER AND LEY

Ley (the main character) excitedly ran to her garden to do gymnastics, like she does every day. She heard a strange noise from underneath her. She put her head against the floor. Suddenly she started sinking into the ground. She was screaming at the top of her lungs, saying, "Help! Help!"

But no one could hear her. She fainted, then after 20 minutes she woke up and saw her best friend. She was really confused and asked, "Summer? What are you doing here?"

"I'm here to ruin your life." Summer said angrily.

Esma Ayguner (11)
Greatfield Park Primary School, Up Hatherley

JOIM, ROOZB AND THE ROBOT

Once upon a time, there was a boy named Joim and his hologram pet named Roozb. They lived in a city that was destroyed, and mostly empty, but there was a giant robot destroying it all with missiles, fire and spikes. Weirdly, Joim and Roozb were never there when the robot was attacking. When the robot was attacking there was a person inside controlling it.

One day when the robot was attacking, a rock flew at the windshield and smashed it open. Surprisingly, inside was Joim controlling the robot. The people were shocked from head to toe.

Mylo Boyle (10)

Greatfield Park Primary School, Up Hatherley

A SUDDEN DEATH

Early sunrise, a weary traveller came to see the king, he was called Zerodeck! He wasn't well known but he came to help King Denis, his best friend. Zerodeck was a beast tamer, the best in the business!

Suddenly, a dragon came from a nearby cliff. Zerodeck seized an artefact attached to a necklace and chanted an incantation. The beast collapsed to the ground in front of him! A gust of wind came from its corpse, knocking him over like a tsunami. The wind flung a sharp arrow in the air - *Bang!* It was all over.

Daniel Wrench (11)

Greatfield Park Primary School, Up Hatherley

WHAT DID THE HERO DO?

Once upon a time, there was a superhero named Captain Rizzle. Captain Rizzle was a popular hero of the galaxy! If you went to Mars you would see every alien watching the news as Captain Rizzle would be on their television.

But one day, after defeating his infamous enemy, Devious Dingle, he gained all the trust of the world. So the FBI gave him a button that, if pressed, would set off a bomb and blow up the solar system. To the dismay of everyone, he pressed the button.

5... 4... 3... 2... 1...

Kaboom!

Noah Birt (11)

Greatfield Park Primary School, Up Hatherley

A STORMY NIGHT

Once upon a time in a long-gone forest, a little girl called Emily walked through the forest to get some bright red apples. Suddenly, an evil witch from the west shot right in front of Emily and threw a bullet at her. She turned Emily into a werewolf. Poor Emily.

When the witch left, the prince of the royal family suddenly saw Emily. He saw her growling. All at once, the prince brought a snow globe. He said, "This is a wish snowglobe, so I wish for you to come back as a girl."

She turned back into a girl.

Rosie McDermott (11)
Greatfield Park Primary School, Up Hatherley

THE MYSTERIOUS FOREST

Wendy and her best friend Enid found themselves in a dark, creepy forest with black, mysterious trees with no leaves, which was extremely muddy. Wendy and Enid went to explore the dark, creepy forest until a little girl appeared.

"Please, help me!" cried the little girl.

Enid and Wendy looked confused, but suddenly the little girl turned into a monster with a sword, for she was a shape-shifter. Enid shrieked! The monster started to fight and Enid got hit, so Wendy started to fight, but then she woke up...

Mia O'Donnell (10)

Greatfield Park Primary School, Up Hatherley

TRAPPED TEDDY BEAR

I, Ted, was squashed and compressed in a full-to-the-brim pencil case. Suddenly, a loud noise went off, shocking the scorching hot classroom. It was getting hotter and hotter until I could see fire through the gap in the compressed pencil case. The classroom was just getting hotter and hotter until the pencil case started burning.

I ran for it, although I risked being seen since I was an alien teddy bear. I ran away to the car park and jumped in a teacher's car as she was driving away whilst children were screaming.

Kian Steed (10)
Greatfield Park Primary School, Up Hatherley

MILA'S TWISTED TALE

I am Mila and my friends are Peter, Sadie and Mary. One day, someone set the school on fire! Everyone was in shock when they found out who did it - Mary! That day, my friends and I were together, except for Mary which was weird since she was always with us. But that was because she was busy setting the school on fire! It turned out she did it because of Mrs Louis. Mary and her have had some tough times, like when she told her to throw away her paper aeroplane which made her very sad. Mary wanted revenge.

Mia Ling (10)
Greatfield Park Primary School, Up Hatherley

EMMA HEARD A ROAR!

As Emma stepped into the corner shop, she heard a roar a couple of miles away, so she ignored it. She went to the shop to get some bread and Lucozade for her mum because she was sick. As Emma left the shop she heard the roar getting louder and louder from the bottom of the road. She ran to the top of the road to get back home. As she looked back, she saw a big, black, stormy monster chasing her. From the bottom of her heart, she thought she was going to be eaten! Then she woke up.

Darcey Curran (10)
Greatfield Park Primary School, Up Hatherley

ALICE AND THE HOLE

Alice was a sweet, innocent girl, however, May, her friend, was not. She would pull her hair and push her in the mud. The pattern never changed. Alice was yet again walking home with messy hair and her skirt covered in mud.

The next day when Alice saw May, she asked if she would go to the forest. May agreed and when they got to the forest Alice excitedly said, "Look! There's a hole!"

Alice pushed May down the hole, then Alice skipped home!

Autumn Cotton-Bettgridge (11)

Greatfield Park Primary School, Up Hatherley

THE FOREST

One day a boy was lost in a forest, his name was Colin. He found a girl called Aimee. They became friends and walked together. When they walked, they thought that they were being watched. As soon as they thought that, they were attacked by a wolf. They ran for their lives, but Colin was too slow and was eaten alive and Aimee fell into a hole and died.

Isaac Chow (10)

Greatfield Park Primary School, Up Hatherley

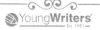
ROB TILL YOU'RE SCARED

"Are we there yet?" Tasha moaned in the car.

"It's only one hour," replied Mum.

"That's so long!"

"Well," said Mum, "there is a shortcut."

"Take it!"

"Okay then."

In a matter of time they were in London. It was now late, so Mum said,

"It's time to rob now!"

In the dead of night they set off. They robbed many houses until they came to a stop. In the darkness, shadows appeared. Tasha hid and out of nowhere, there were red shoes, a spotty shirt, and green hair. It was a clown and they froze in horror immediately.

Maeve Moran (7)

Holland Junior School, Hurst Green

WHEN THE IMPOSSIBLE BECOMES POSSIBLE

"The crowd roars as Kylian Mbappé scores his one-thousandth goal for PSG, this is incredible. Mbappé is clearly the best player in the world. Hopefully, his reign can last forever."

Next match for Mbappé, would Mbappé break his streak by not scoring a hat-trick? Probably not because he was unstoppable. But little did he know something unthinkable would happen...

"Mbappé on the ball, he dribbles down the wing. Why did he stop? Is-is his skin turning green? Is he an alien? Oh my gosh, is he eating all his teammates? I think he is coming to eat me..."

Leo Messi (10)

Holland Junior School, Hurst Green

JENNY'S SECRET

Bang! Crash! Smash! Tables and chairs flew across the classroom. The children panicked and the teacher screamed as Chocolate, the class hamster, went sailing through the air. The whiteboard went soaring across the class and... *Bang!* While the children ran for cover, Jenny just sat there quietly, watching, waiting. What her classmates didn't know, but would find out soon enough, was that Jenny had a magic power! Jenny was able to move things with her eyes. And from now until the end of term, Jenny had decided that every Friday afternoon she would cause absolute chaos in Holly class.

Evalyn Casey (7)
Holland Junior School, Hurst Green

AWFUL MOTHER

Zoe lives in Alaska and has an awful stepmum with a pet eagle. One day her father dies suddenly and the next day a chimney sweep rings at the door. The stepmother is suspicious, so when the sweep is cleaning the fireplace - *boom!* She lights the fire. He scrambles and climbs but he is too late.
Zoe tries to save him until... her awful stepmother explains it all. "I killed your father and he was a chimney sweep himself. I knew he didn't die at all."
"What?" said Zoe. "So you're saying the chimney sweep was my father?"
"Yes, child."

Jessica Dean (9)
Holland Junior School, Hurst Green

THE GOOD DEED

It was a snowy Christmas Eve. Dave looked out of his window and noticed a silhouette shivering in the moonlight. Dave opened the door and shouted, "Come in out of the cold!"

When they were inside, Dave left the fellow by the blazing fire to warm up whilst he went to make hot chocolate for them both. Dave came back after a few minutes to find the fellow was gone!

"He's left my house a mess! Water on the floor and clothes everywhere!"

Dave was confused until he saw the carrot...

"Silly me!" laughed Dave. "I should've worn my glasses!"

Freddy Seyit (10)

Holland Junior School, Hurst Green

THE TWISTS AND TURNS OF CHRISTMAS

Bang! Emily and Buddy ran downstairs. Their elf on the shelf was on the floor with a glowing bag of sweets next to him! Emily and Buddy looked at each other - "Just one," they said, but as they ate they felt dizzy. Everything went black.

When they opened their eyes they saw a man wearing a red and white cloak. Emily and Buddy knew who it was... Santa Claus! He smiled warmly at them.

"I've been expecting you two!" Their mouths were wide open. "Come on, let's save Christmas for everyone!"

Jumping on the reindeer, they flew into the night!

Neve O'Neill (10)

Holland Junior School, Hurst Green

A WACKY TRAIN JOURNEY!

It was another buzzing day at the train station, like a swarm of bees protecting their hive. One particular train that was due to stop at the bustling train station was approaching too fast. Was the train going to stop? What about those passengers on the train?

Many people in the busy train station stood there watching like statues. The train came to a screeching halt as smoke ballooned from the underside of the train. *Phew!* Eventually, the railway station became desolate and quiet except for the hissing, electrified line, which sounded like slithering snakes having a celebration.

Francesca Arcidiacono (9)

Holland Junior School, Hurst Green

SEEING YOUR DREAMS THE WRONG WAY AROUND

Once there was a boy called Tom. Tom loved dinosaurs. He really wanted to be a palaeontologist when he grew up. One day he went to his history club. It was the only subject he liked. When he arrived, the classroom was empty. He realised that he could poke around. He went to the supply room and, *fwoom!* He then saw some prehistoric plants.

"Yes!" he said. "I can finally see a dinosaur!"

But then he smelt a putrid scent. He looked behind him and, "Ahhh!"

A tyrannosaurus rex was there sinking his knife-sharp teeth into Tom's helpless body.

Dominic Kromalicki (10)

Holland Junior School, Hurst Green

ZOMBIE ATTACK

My name is Bobby and this is my story. One bright morning, I was walking through the woods when a bunch of zombies started attacking ferociously. I had to run. I wasn't looking where I was going, so I fell into a flowing river.

I managed to climb out but the zombies had caught up with me, and they were surrounding me. Their three eyes were glowing red like blood. They were getting closer and closer to me. I was just about to jump when... Game over!

"This level's hard!" I said.

"Turn it off," said Mum. "It's bathtime anyway."

Joseph Levin (8)
Holland Junior School, Hurst Green

MAGIC

It was the first day of school. Melanie bumped into two girls, Harmony and Melody. They were identical twins. One had glasses.

A few weeks later the girls found a pen. Melanie thought it was no ordinary pen. She drew an umbrella and suddenly one appeared out of thin air.

Wow, thought the twins. They were amazed. "We need that."

So when Melanie was in class, the twins snuck quietly to her locker and swapped the pen with an ordinary one. The twins tried to draw different things, but nothing happened. Then they realised it was Melanie who was magic!

Mia Kimber (9)

Holland Junior School, Hurst Green

TIME TRAVEL

This is Alex. Alex loves Lego, drawing and science. He recently found out about a scientist who thinks he's able to invent time travel. This might sound amazing, but it's not, and here's why.

The time machine failed; it tore the fabric of time and eventually destroyed the universe. In other words, it was never supposed to be real. He had to confront him.

The next week, Alex went to the first test and was really embarrassed. I can't say the whole conversation because I only have 100 words. Anyway, it worked. Alex was then seen as a hero forever.

Archie Alexander (10)

Holland Junior School, Hurst Green

LAKELAND ADVENTURE

In Lakeland lived a well-loved ogre, a lonely, scary giant and a villainous wizard that yearned for power and set a curse on the ogre. Scared, everyone ran from the ogre. The wizard proclaimed, "You can be happy if you vanquish the giant!"

The brave ogre found the giant and told him the wizard's plot. The giant was fuming when he heard. The giant snatched the wizard's wand and squashed him, breaking the curse.

The giant became best friends with the ogre and became a hero in Lakeland when the news spread. Now the wizard can't strike evil.

Benjamin Jones (9)
Holland Junior School, Hurst Green

THE THREE LITTLE PIGS

Once upon a time, there were three little pigs, one busy mummy pig and one big, bad wolf. One particular morning, she said to the pigs, "I'm so busy, please build your own houses!"

One hour later the houses were built and they had moved in. Along came the big bad wolf. He tried to blow down all three houses, which made the pigs cross, so they told him off.

"Don't be angry," said the big bad wolf. "I was feeling lonely and wanted some friends to play football with."

So they all had a fun game of football together.

Tommy England (7)
Holland Junior School, Hurst Green

HAPPILY EVER AFTER

Unfortunately for Rapunzel and the prince, their happily ever after had backfired. This is because Rapunzel had disobeyed Mother Gothel's order. After this happened, Mother decided she wanted to get revenge, so she kidnapped the prince and locked him away in her tower with no way to escape. The prince was trapped.

Enough was enough for Rapunzel, so she went to the tower to rescue the prince. Mother Gothel had left the tower so Rapunzel quickly lassoed her hair up to the prince and lowered him to the ground. Is this finally happily ever after?

Cleo Wyatt (8)
Holland Junior School, Hurst Green

STAR GYMNAST

Amy carefully rubbed some chalk on her shaking hands. Taking a deep breath, she presented towards the judges. Quiet descended on the arena and she was off! Amy is a world-class gymnast and the bars are her very best event. She always scored higher than anybody else.

Amy was halfway through her routine and doing exceptionally well. *Bang!* Everyone gasped, she was a heap on the floor! Amy was devastated! She rubbed her eyes. Then suddenly, the audience began to vanish! Amy was confused; what was going on? And then it hit her, it was all a dream!

Evelyn Butcher (9)
Holland Junior School, Hurst Green

STITCH AND ANGEL IN PARIS

Once upon a time, there were two aliens named Stitch and Angel. They were siblings. They lived at Disneyland Paris.

One day, they bought a teddy and it suddenly disappeared. They both worked as a team to find the teddy. They searched everywhere apart from the castle which was guarded by the horrible Lady Gothel. Both Stitch and Angel worked together to gain special powers to freeze Gothel so that they could enter the castle. They were finally able to enter the castle. They found the teddy and quickly escaped before Gothel unfroze and went back home.

Taya Steptoe (8)
Holland Junior School, Hurst Green

THE MYSTERIOUS METEOR

Today, when I was watching cartoons, the news automatically turned on. I tried to change the channel but it said it got cancelled, so I listened to the news and it said: "Breaking news! A meteor has been spotted by a satellite and we only have five minutes until it comes crashing down to Earth!"

My mum and dad worried in the kitchen while my brother and sister were panicking in the playroom. Then, after five minutes we could see the meteor. It was metres from the ground.

Then a UFO came and sucked it up and rapidly flew away.

Rosie Mann (9)

Holland Junior School, Hurst Green

JUST HORSING AROUND

Saturday night was always a big night at the Farmer's Arms pub and tonight was no exception. Ready to be up at the crack of dawn, Old Macdonald put all his animals to bed early, but the animals were having none of it.

As soon as the sunshine dipped below the horizon, the pub was open for business. Horace the horse walked in and plonked himself on a barstool that creaked under his weight and his size, his big lips making slurping noises.

The bartender gave him a jug of apple juice and said, "Hi Horace, why the long face?"

Alex Hall (9)

Holland Junior School, Hurst Green

THE MYSTERIOUS WORLD

Once upon a time, a young, 10-year-old boy named Liam and his twin sister, Anna, were going to bed. They both woke up at the same time for school. Mum and Dad were still sleeping but they did what they needed to do and got on the school bus. This time, the driver was a cartoon deer. Anna ran to him and said, "Aww!"

Liam stood there and said, "Let's go!"

Everyone had changed into animals. When they arrived at school they got sent home. Everyone at school was an animal but then they woke up for real.

Kaydra Darko (9)
Holland Junior School, Hurst Green

DUDE BECOMES A GOOD GUY

Dude was a Las Vegas bad guy and he had an enemy called Freezan. They got into a lot of battles which were ruining the city. Everyone begged them to stop but they never listened.

During one of their epic battles, Dude saw a building start to fall down with a child under it, so he sprinted to the child to save them immediately. Everyone thought Dude was going to hurt the child, which made him upset but he proved them wrong and helped instead.

The child said, "Thank you! You're not such a bad guy after all!"

Benjamin Carman (9)

Holland Junior School, Hurst Green

FAME

Victor Vlogger was an 8-year-old who wanted to be the most famous YouTuber in the world. No matter how many videos he uploaded, he couldn't get any subscribers.

He got tangled up in his lead and he fell face-first into dog poop. Unfortunately, someone managed to catch it on camera. They uploaded it to YouTube and overnight Victor gained the same subscribers as MrBeast, the most famous YouTuber.

Then, all of a sudden, one more subscriber, which was King Charles. Now Victor was the most famous YouTuber in the world.

Buddy Krol (8)
Holland Junior School, Hurst Green

DANCE PARTY

There once was a famous dancing chicken called Diane, who had a sidekick cat called Socks. One day, Diane went to record one of her dance videos but her computer had been stolen. Diane grabbed her magic carpet and flew off to find it.

She zoomed through clouds and came across a fox called Boa, who had taken her computer. Diane began to dance to distract Boa, but to her surprise, the fox began to dance too. He was a magnificent dancer. Diane invited Boa to be her dance partner and they went on to win lots of trophies.

Louis Swindells
Holland Junior School, Hurst Green

JOSH'S DREAM

One day in an enormous, lush, green garden, Josh was playing Pokémon. He left the TV on and walked in the house and *bang* he was transported into the TV and he appeared in the game he was playing. In the game, he spawned in the wild area right next to a Torcal and he had one Pokéball, so he caught the Torkoal and it was registered to his Pokédex. He didn't even know he had a Pokédex. He was having a great time but he saw that everything was fading away and he woke up from dreaming.

Benjamin Whitelock (9)

Holland Junior School, Hurst Green

PICKLE AND CHARLIE

Two monkeys were walking in the wood. They found a house that looked pretty good, covered in chocolate and gummies. They gobbled them all in their tummies.

Inside lived a witch with a small ginger cat who she used as a trap to punish monkeys who stole her sweets and put them in a pie with meat.

The cat had a plan of his own. He hated eating monkey's bones. He used her book of spells that was meant to turn her into a jellybean. It didn't quite work out, but at least he got something nice in his mouth.

Tabitha Windett (7)
Holland Junior School, Hurst Green

A DUCK NAMED DUCK

Once there was a duck named Duck. Duck was having breakfast and met a cow named Cow, and just like that they became the best of friends. The cow explained that his mum had turned into a piano. Duck felt bad for Cow, so asked if he would show him.

"Moo," replied Cow.

It took three days, but when they got there, Duck was amazed at the piano. Cow asked if Duck had any idea how to turn her back. But Duck didn't hear Cow, as he was laughing too much at the piano, knowing he'd turned her into it!

Freddie Funnell (10)

Holland Junior School, Hurst Green

THE FOX FINDS NEW FRIENDS

One day a fox called Mary went far away from her home where her mother also lived. She suddenly found a new spruce forest and a tiny, stripey thing. It was quite shy, so she asked, "Are you okay?"

It said, "Yes, I am fine," in a very quiet and squeaky voice.

"Do you want to be friends?" Mary asked.

"Yes," it answered.

Mary followed it through the spruce and they found a cat who wasn't shy and wanted to be friends. They were all friends and it felt great!

Alexis Thomas-Morris (10)
Holland Junior School, Hurst Green

A SPACE ADVENTURE

Our class went on a coach to a space museum; we were very excited. When we got there we were astonished at how ginormous it was.

A guide opened a simulator for us. We saw Mars on the screen, then we opened the door and outside the ground was red. We looked at our teacher, he'd turned into an alien! He was wearing the same yellow, spotty tie.

Then our coach flew to us to take us back to school. Our headteacher asked where Mr Brown was but we didn't think he would believe us so we said he'd quit.

Emily Buckham (7)

Holland Junior School, Hurst Green

THE UNKNOWN STRANGER ABOUT TO BE CAUGHT!

Yesterday, something unexpected happened. I was walking down the street, heading home after a busy day at work. As I just arrived, I glanced at someone begging for money and a home. I felt incredibly generous as it was nearly Christmas, so I offered for him to stay in my house for a few weeks.

Before I knew it, it had been three days with him in my house. I noticed a few things had gone missing from my house while I was at work, so I questioned him; he was faking being homeless all along, just to steal!

Demi Oosthuizen (10)

Holland Junior School, Hurst Green

THE MYSTERY

Once upon a day lived me, Iris. It was the first day back at school after an extremely exciting summer. I was walking along when I noticed that all the lovely plants and wildlife were gone! My heart started to race, so I lifted my feet to tell everyone at school.

School was different too because when I walked in everyone and everything was frozen. I realised they were too scared to solve this mystery. I shouted, "Let's get to work and solve climate change!"

So that's what we did.

Isobel Eltringham (9)

Holland Junior School, Hurst Green

BUTTERCUP, THE MOUSE AND THE WOLF

The big scary wolf lived in a big scary cave, and a small creature came into the cave without the big scary wolf noticing. The big scary wolf saw that creature and that creature was a little sad mouse, so the wolf did not eat the mouse, he helped the sad mouse. The mouse was scared at first, then saw that the wolf was trying to help and was not going to eat her so they became best friends and they adventured into a magic forest. They saw a fairy called Buttercup and they all became best friends forever.

Tillie Sene (7)

Holland Junior School, Hurst Green

INTO THE DEEP

Jack went fishing with his dad on a riverbank. Jack caught a huge fish. He tried to reel it in but the fish was too strong. It pulled Jack into the river. It swam deeper and deeper and Jack ran out of breath. He let go of the fishing rod and sank to the bottom.

He woke up in an underwater cave with a mermaid by his side. She'd saved his life. Her name was Willow. She wanted to keep Jack but knew he wouldn't survive in her underwater world so she sadly swam with him back to the riverbank.

Summer Smith (9)
Holland Junior School, Hurst Green

LOST

"I think I'm lost!" Fred cried. As he wandered he nervously peeked around a tree and made eye contact with a huge, hairy ogre! Frantically sprinting away, dodging trees, he fell into a dark pit.

Blinking his eyes, he woke up face-to-face with the ogre! Dangling a stick into the pit, the monster was trying to get out of the hole. The monster directed him out of the forest and they both walked to Fred's house safely. Then, because Fred was so shocked, they became friends.

Matthew Mitrovic (10)

Holland Junior School, Hurst Green

PURRFECT PRIME MINISTER

Once upon a time, there was a cat called Kia. Kia's dream was to be the Prime Minister, but the problem was, Kia is a cat and cats can't be the Prime Minister. The next month or two there was an election and Kia really wanted to enter, so he did.

The next day the election was ready and Kia won, and he was the Prime Minister for a long time, but everyone seemed to think it was a mistake to let Kia be the Prime Minister because he was bossy, annoying and loud, so Kia lost his job.

Ada Kelly (10)
Holland Junior School, Hurst Green

THE BOOK

I was reading in bed when the book started sucking me in, I appeared in a forest, dark and grim. I saw a wooden cottage nearby. Being my nosy self I took a peek inside. A dark, drab wolf was about to kill its prey. Luckily I was there to save the day!

I tackled the beast with my bare hands and took the wolf to the ground. I cut its fat belly open and Grandma was what I found! Little Red and Grandma thanked me and offered me some tea. I had some cake as well, it was yummy!

Daisy Mann (9)
Holland Junior School, Hurst Green

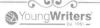

THE THREE LITTLE STUDENTS AND THE BIG BAD TEACHER!

Once upon a time, there were three kids, Nell, Belle and Lottie. They loved school, that was until the big bad teacher arrived. Not only was she bad, she was pure evil! She hated all children and made them do lots of horrid chores.

One day, Nell, Belle and Lottie had had enough, so they locked her in the cupboard and she is still there to this day!

Nell Kelly (8)
Holland Junior School, Hurst Green

RUBY AND THE WOLF

"Ahhh!" Ruby screamed as the wolf came out of the bushes on the path.

"Oh, sorry," said the wolf. "Where are you off to?"

"I'm going to my grandmother's house."

"I shall come with you because there is a big bad... chicken!"

"Oh no," said Ruby. "We should be careful."

As they were walking, they heard something in the bushes.

"Be quiet," said Ruby. "I hear something."

It was the big... bad... chicken!

"Ruuun!"

They ran as fast as their legs would take them, and in the end, they made it to Ruby's grandmother's - well, the wolf did.

Jessica Taylor (10)

Mintlaw Primary School, Mintlaw

A BLAST FROM THE FUTURE

Back in prehistoric times when the meteor was about to hit Earth, time stopped. While the dinosaurs were strangely thinking about what happened they got time-warped 10 quadrillion years later. There were robots everywhere. They were flabbergasted about their surroundings. Then the unexpected happened. They got warped 100 decillion years later on Mars. John Beanos and Elias Muskateer were there and there were flying pandas, swimming giraffes and walking sharks. Everything you once knew was gone. It was like Earth but very rusty. Every single piece was gone, just a brown, pale dot with cities, towns, countries, continents, farms and villages.

Reuben Price (10)

Mintlaw Primary School, Mintlaw

THE KING'S CASTLE

A boy named William falls into a portal! It whizzes him into an old-looking giant hall, with cracked pillars like they are going to crumble.

"Where am I?" William questions.

He hears static, then a friendly voice saying, "Welcome to stage one of the Death Traps! If you survive this, you can meet us in the throne room."

What does he mean by death traps? thinks William.

Suddenly he hears, "Congratulations, you have completed stage one, you may now meet us!"

In the throne room, William sees a tall, brown-haired man who says in a deep voice, "Welcome..."

Michael Burke (10)

Mintlaw Primary School, Mintlaw

CINDERELLA

One gloomy afternoon, a girl who was fed up with her mum walked into a creepy wood. At the end of the woods she saw a rusty cabin. She went in and saw a fairy godmother. The fairy godmother said, "What's your name, dear?"

The girl answered, "I am Cinderella. And you are?"

The Fairy godmother said, "I am a fairy godmother, mwah."

Cinderella said, "Nice to meet you, could you make me look beautiful?"

The fairy godmother flicked her wand. Cinderella went to see herself and touched the mirror. Suddenly she was in a weird space dimension...

Demi-Rose Parry (10)

Mintlaw Primary School, Mintlaw

THE EXPLOSION

In 1614, a captain named Bob was a bull! His passengers were aliens. The passengers were petrified, as well as the captain and his crew, who were speechless. Petrified, they heard a thunderous *bang!* They were all horrified. They felt vibrations. They all leapt out. The captain had exploded! He sent all the passengers through a portal.

One of the passengers said emotionally, "Where, oh where are we!?"

One started having a mental breakdown until they crashed into an iceberg! The aliens bumped right into ice people and they all lived together, happily, icily ever after.

Alayah McLeod (10)
Mintlaw Primary School, Mintlaw

SNOW WHITE WITH A TWIST

One day a kind stepmother called Stella was doing chores at home when she knocked over a vase. Stella's evil stepdaughter Snow White kicked her out of her home with no food. Stella wandered, cold and alone for hours until she found a little house. She knocked on the door and went inside... When the owner came home, he angrily shouted, "Get out of my house!" So Stella ran away crying. She ran and ran until she found herself at a castle. "Wow this is amazing!" exclaimed Stella.

"Finally, you woke up!" said the prince. "Now what do we do...?"

Isla Elrick (10)

Mintlaw Primary School, Mintlaw

ALIENS ON THE MOON!

One horrifying day there was an explosion on the famous space explorer's spaceship causing it to crash land on a planet. Posey and Jeffery used their old ship to build a new craft to fly around. While exploring the main island on the new world, they found aliens already there. So now Posey and Jeffery needed to defend themselves because the aliens were not friendly!

Posey and Jeffery started talking to the aliens and found out that they liked to play spaceball; so instead of fighting they played spaceball against each other and shared the alien world peacefully.

Cooper Leslie (10)

Mintlaw Primary School, Mintlaw

THE THREE LITTLE PIGS

Once upon a time, there were three little pigs and a big black wolf. They were all best friends. The wolf lived in a cottage and the three little pigs lived in three mansions. They had one each. The mansions were worth over four million pounds each. Meanwhile, the little pigs called a meeting in one of the three houses. After they gathered around the table for a moment, there was silence. Then one of the pigs said, "We are being selfish." "How?" said the other one.

"We are buying all this stuff and the wolf only has a cottage..."

Millie Hunter (10)
Mintlaw Primary School, Mintlaw

HUMPTY DUMPTY AND THE GREAT WALL OF CHINA

One day, Humpty Dumpty is on a trip to the Great Wall of China. He feels hands on his back and the next thing he knows he's falling off the Great Wall of China. He thinks it's over, but when he lands he falls onto a random island.

On the island is a massive forest. As he's exploring, he hears random talking and goes near and is behind a masked man, likely in a tribe.

A decade passes, three-quarters of the boat's finished. Humpty Dumpty's teaching kids and the bell rings. The next day a wave destroys all. It's sunk.

Subhan Anwar (10)

Mintlaw Primary School, Mintlaw

THURSDAY

Once upon a time, there was a girl called Thursday, she and her friends moved into a new house that was haunted.

They unpacked all their things into their new rooms. Bionca went into the living room and shut the door. She said, "Nobody come in!"

Later, she unlocked the door and everyone started singing Happy Birthday because Bionca had organised a surprise party for Thursday.

Thursday got her presents and opened them. They were new clothes. "Thank you guys!" she said with a smile. They all lived happily ever.

Indi Taylor (10)
Mintlaw Primary School, Mintlaw

BATTLE OF FRASERBURGH

France had been captured by Germany. They had almost got all the UK, except for Mintlaw. The British were sending supplies to the USSR and the Germans did not like that! So, 1,200 planes were sent to stop the plan in Fraserburgh RAF base from interfering. The bombers went overhead.
We waited for the last to go. We climbed into the cockpits of our Spitfires. We got to Fraserburgh, 100 bombers were coming from the sun! We started the fight, they got shots on the ships, then there were five left! They got a taste of their own medicine!

Archie Henderson (10)
Mintlaw Primary School, Mintlaw

ON THE MOON

The characters are Captain America and Timmy the Triangle. The place is set in space, near the Milky Way. Soon, they find a magical portal that leads to the moon.

When they get to the moon, they find aliens. Timmy the Triangle starts shooting at the aliens with an assault rifle and submariner guns. Eventually, the aliens get tired of it so they start shooting back with rocket launchers and miniguns and they shoot holes in the ship. Then it falls so quickly!

When they get home, they find their family are actually aliens too.

Hayden Reid (9)
Mintlaw Primary School, Mintlaw

FRIDAY

One stormy morning Friday, a detective, was searching the forest for clues because a naughty clown had been seen there.

Friday came across the clown being silly in the woods and realised she didn't recognise the clown. So, Friday sneaked off to the sheriff's office and told him what she had seen. He left the room for a minute and the naughty clown came into the room and chased her away!

Quickly Friday ran off screaming and the police officers arrested the sheriff because he was the naughty clown after all!

Isla Robbie (10)
Mintlaw Primary School, Mintlaw

THREE BIG CAVE PIGS VS HUMANS

Once, there were three big cave pigs. They searched for a cave. They found a cave and sang a song about caves. "Caves are our home, they are nice and cosy! We love our home!"
Suddenly they bumped into cave pigs and they planned to take over the world and celebrate. They found lots of yummy food from the shops but the humans planned to take it back.
Surprisingly it took the humans a while to get the world back, it took them 2 years and 36 hours. Then the humans ate the pigs and they sang a lovely song.

Cammie Chan (10)
Mintlaw Primary School, Mintlaw

THE EARTHQUAKE

There was a boy called Eren. His mum sent him to get food because she was hungry. So, he got food from the supermarket then went back home. Tired, he gave it to his mum and went to wait for his friend at a huge wall.

Eren met his friend there they talked for a while until they heard rumbling. It was an earthquake! Then the ground split and a black substance came up, they screamed an ear-splitting scream. Suddenly, they flew up into the air to safety then saw they were really puppets getting played with!

Charlie Watt (9)

Mintlaw Primary School, Mintlaw

THE SNUCK-OUT SISTER

There are three elements who live on the moon. One is called Sage, she's a fire element. Saule is a girl and is a water element. Vaickas is an air element, he's the dad of the elements. There's just one more element and she is just a baby. Her name is Evelyn and she is the earth element. She is only five months old and Sage and Saule are not happy. So Sage thinks to sneak out, even though her dad told her not to, and at midnight she packs her bags and then sneaks out when everyone is asleep...

Ugne Skersyte (10)
Mintlaw Primary School, Mintlaw

THE BOAT THAT GOT HIT BY A TREE

There were 20,000 passengers on the Titanic and they were on a day cruise and having a party. They were sailing for hours and hours and loved to party.

Helana and Erin were sleeping, Aimee and Scott were having breakfast and the rest were in the pool. For the next hour, they were all eating lunch and playing in the pool, having fun.

Suddenly a massive tree hit the ship and the ship was sinking. Twenty-one passengers had a secret, they were all dolphins! So they swam to Dolphin Land and had fun.

Alyssia Dawson (10)
Mintlaw Primary School, Mintlaw

BIG WEB

Once, there was a spider, but it was not tiny, it was big. Gigantic, in fact! It couldn't climb the drain because it was too big. It had to climb up the side! While it was climbing a ball flew at it. It had time to react, so it jumped away. Eventually, it found a window and investigated it. There was a man in that room. The window was open, so it climbed in. It jumped on the man. "Argh!" he shouted, frightened! It turned out he was a zookeeper so he took the spider to live at the zoo.

Joseph Macmillan (10)
Mintlaw Primary School, Mintlaw

TITANIC SHIP DISASTER

All the passengers were getting onto the ship. They were so excited to go on their holiday. The boat was called Titanic, they thought it was weird but they stayed on the boat. Little did they know there was an alien trying to kill everyone.

A little girl hid in the toilets. She was scared; she needed to find a way to fix this. She crawled across the floor to try and escape but she was a little too late. She was able to defeat the aliens on board and got a medal from the Queen.

Zoey Jamieson (10)
Mintlaw Primary School, Mintlaw

THE THREE LITTLE WOLVES

One beautiful day, Big Pig was having a walk in the forest and found the three little wolves' houses, made out of brick, leather and wood. Big Pig went to the brick house first and, to be honest, I'm quite surprised by what Big Pig did. Well, he hit the house with a sledgehammer and then ate the wolf! Then he decided to ride a lion into the leather house. Swiftly moving on, he ran into the wood house.

Then Big Wolf came and roasted Big Pig and ate him! He was hungry.

Hamish Bream (10)

Mintlaw Primary School, Mintlaw

TITANIC ALIENS VS WEIRD HUMANS

Everyone gets on board the fascinating boat and then it hits a slippery iceberg and starts to float up into space. It's now in space and it's floating up to the moon. The passengers are aliens so they go to their homes.

They eventually get back on the ship to go back to Earth. They get hit by a gigantic meteorite and go speeding down to Earth. They crash land and get up for a bit, but then a virus comes and they all die! The aliens' plan had been foiled.

Jacob Mayhew (10)
Mintlaw Primary School, Mintlaw

CHERNOBYL

People heard an explosion and they went to see what it was. They went to the reactor and it had exploded and what came out? Cotton candy. Everyone was confused, then something was in the sky. Everyone saw it. It was a UFO. They landed and aliens came out!

They had to evacuate the city by bus, car and foot. Someone put down an indestructible bubble covering Chernobyl so all the cotton candy and aliens are trapped for life.

Daniel Milne (10)
Mintlaw Primary School, Mintlaw

SCHOOL TRIP

One day, Mia and Darcy woke up, excited for a school trip to the farm. They quickly put on their shoes and headed out the door.

When they got to school, the bus was waiting outside. The bus was coloured as bright as the sun. They arrived almost immediately. Mia ran straight to the horses. She was leaning against the brown wooden fence and *bang!* Suddenly, the horses were out!

"Chase after them!" said Darcy.

Mia chased the horses over high fences and fast choppy rivers and finally caught them eating apples.

"I'm going to be in trouble," said Mia.

Lily Lewis (10)
Shifnal Primary School, Shifnal

THE TALKING CHEESTRING

There was a plain old Cheestring, but not for long...
There was a boy called Riley, he was eating a
Cheestring and I was the Cheestring.
The worst thing was, he was in school when it
happened.
I burst out, "Don't eat my head!"
Everybody screamed, "It's a talking Cheestring!"
Riley didn't know what was happening. "A talking
Cheestring?" Riley didn't know what to do, but
then he passed out.
Riley then woke up from the horrible dream.
He went to school and guess what happened?
The Cheestring was talking!

Isla-Rose Wootton (10)
Shifnal Primary School, Shifnal

THAT DREADFUL DAY

Boom! I could hear explosions everywhere. "Where are you?" I heard my friend Benjamin say. I lay there motionless. I could hear the endless sounds of sirens and people shouting. I had just been hit by a Russian missile and was bleeding uncontrollably. I couldn't believe I had been hit, and I strongly believed I was dying. Miraculously, I survived.

My family, Benjamin, his family and I moved away after our town was bombed, but we were still haunted by the disastrous events of the dreadful day on which many died on the 19th January 1969.

Jessie Zhao
Shifnal Primary School, Shifnal

THE TELEPORTATION

One normal night, Maya was getting ready for bed, but she said in her head, "I'm so hungry, I just don't want to walk downstairs. I wish I could teleport." The next day she woke up still hungry, but she wasn't allowed downstairs yet.

"Teleport me downstairs," she said, and the next thing she knew, she was downstairs.

"OMG!" she said. "Did I just teleport?"

"Teleport me to my room!" she commanded.

She ate the food and went straight back to sleep for when her parents came to wake her up.

Ruby White (10)
Shifnal Primary School, Shifnal

MOLLY AND IDA: THE DISAPPEARANCE OF IDA

"I got you into a school! One of those schools that you sleep at!"

"A boarding school," I mumbled from under the covers.

She smacked me, my evil stepmother.

Great, I thought, as I opened my eyes.

I got up and she dashed into Ida's room. I presumed that she was going to say the same thing. But she ran back into my room. "Ida's gone!" she laughed.

I gasped and I sprinted into her room. I tripped on the way, but I was fine. I pulled down the covers and there she was. I breathed a sigh of relief.

Maggie Barnes
Shifnal Primary School, Shifnal

PIGS IN BLANKETS

The air turned to smoke. Struggling to breathe, I saw my dad through the mist, wafting a tea towel below the smoke alarm. All of a sudden, something jumped out at me. They were pigs! Not just ordinary pigs, they were wearing blankets of all different colours. Purple, green, orange, you name it!

Realising what had just happened, I got up and saw the pigs waddle into the local corner shop. "Stop those pigs!" came a voice from behind. Knocking every tin can off the shelves and onto the... *Bang!* Gunshots rang. What a disaster!

Betsy Simpson (11)
Shifnal Primary School, Shifnal

THE WOLF AND THE FOX

Once upon a time, in 1906, a wolf and a fox became best friends. It started when Lia was strolling through the forest looking for her dinner, and suddenly the bushes started to shake. Slowly, Lia lunged towards the bushes, thinking it might be a squirrel that she could eat for dinner. However, as soon as Lia got too close to the bushes, a little fox popped out and said, "Hello, my name's Gwen. I lost my mum a week ago and ever since I've been hiding here."

"Okay," Lia said, and she promised she would look after her forever.

Aoife Boden (9)
Shifnal Primary School, Shifnal

THE WHITE ROOM

Exactly three days ago, Charlotte was walking down the palace gardens when something hit her. It was a small pebble.

"Who threw that?" she shouted.

Charlotte caught a glimpse of a figure in the window. At first, she thought it was a small child, but after another look, she saw something else but wasn't sure what it could be.

After a lot of chasing, Charlotte thought she saw the figure open a small door and run in. Charlotte crouched through the door. She found herself inside a blank, white room. But the door had gone...

Emma Heritage-Owen (10)
Shifnal Primary School, Shifnal

HEDGEHOG EATS A SAUSAGE

One day, Hedgehog was bored. He wanted to go to the 'Big BBQ Fair' but had no way of getting there. He decided to try and walk for a while. He walked and walked until he got tired. He didn't know how he could get there, but then a seagull flew down from the sky and said, "Come on, I'll fly you there!"

Hedgehog was happy and they reached the fair successfully. They soon found the barbecue, and as they didn't want to be spotted, he hurriedly grabbed a sausage and shared it with the seagull. Hedgehog is very happy.

Harriet Goodchild
Shifnal Primary School, Shifnal

MURDER

He didn't mean to kill her. It was an accident. He had just spun around with the knife in his hand and struck her. Right in the heart.

He had run. He ran until his little legs couldn't run anymore. The sound of the ambulance came closer and closer each time his heart beat. Maybe he wouldn't be sent to jail. After all, there was no proof. But then he reasoned, not every child killed their own mum.

After what seemed like hours, he got up. He turned himself in to the police, explaining everything. They put him behind bars.

Dhron Narender-Rajan
Shifnal Primary School, Shifnal

THE VAMPIRE NEXT DOOR

One grey afternoon, Lila saw a strange man move in next door. She saw a glimpse of him. He looked different to a normal person. Lila told her mum she was going out.

Her mum said, "Okay, be safe."

Lila went next door. The blinds were closed. The floorboards were broken. She tiptoed upstairs. The stairs were creaking when she went into the bedroom. She saw a vampire, so she opened the blinds and the vampire opened his eyes. The vampire screeched and died.

It was all nice and lovely, everything was fixed.

Lillian Whitfield

Shifnal Primary School, Shifnal

HORRIBLE EGYPT

If you like history, you will like this story.

On 21st November 1823, there were two unknown men stuck in a pyramid. They were stuck far away from the king. The king was scared of being alone. The men were used as slaves. One day, they had a thought to break free. They were sick of being told what to do. They made a hammer out of stone to chisel their way out. It didn't work.

They thought, *that's it.*

Until they had a bright idea! They ran through the gate that was open day and night.

Jamie Broome (9)
Shifnal Primary School, Shifnal

WAR OF THE SEAGULLS

Every day the seagulls woke up to thousands of dead birds. After a month of war, the beach was such a mess. Suddenly the leader bird got shot and his blood poured into the sea. The sea turned red. Blood attracts sharks. The king shark jumped out of the sea with its mouth wide open and crash-landed on the sand. The shark gasped for breath. The world is now a dump with a brown sky, a green sun, yellow seas, orange grass and plants that eat people.

Squawk war.

Who will be next to die?

Elsie Clewes
Shifnal Primary School, Shifnal

THE LOST WORLD

One night, me and my pet dog were sleeping in my cabin. Suddenly, there was a *bang!* Me and my dog went to check it out. It was a portal. We went into it and found an ocean. My dog was drowning in the water, so we headed to shore. I said to my dog, "There is a rock stuck in the tree."

So me and my dog tried to get the rock out, but it wasn't moving. Then we found a man talking, but when we got there, there was no one. Me and my dog asked, "What happened?"

Harry Hemsley (10)
Shifnal Primary School, Shifnal

THE DRAMA

At an underwater hotel, there was one person living inside. His name was Jon and he was a frog. He was tall. But then another person came in. He was a fish. Jon went down to have a closer look at him. Neither of them liked the other and they started to fight.

The employees ran upstairs and watched on the stairs. The employees were scared but then they looked around the room and found a shield. They charged into battle, but they stopped because Jon and the fish were having a handshake.

Alfie

Shifnal Primary School, Shifnal

SANTA

One night, Santa was on his sleigh and his reindeer were pulling it. He was going to the last house to deliver the very last present, but this house had lights on.

Santa was thinking that it was the middle of the night and everyone should be asleep, then all the lights turned off. Santa went down the chimney and delivered the present to a kind little girl.

Then he was all done and finished delivering all the presents. Now he is going back to his house, ready for Christmas Day.

Megan Garbett

Shifnal Primary School, Shifnal

JACK THE GIANT

One day there was a giant in the town, his name was Jack. He was one of the meanest giants ever. It was a normal day when he decided to attack the little town next to his house.

So he grabbed his hammer and he went on his way to destroy the little town.

When he got there, all the people were ready for battle. They all had spoons and he was not getting past. They started climbing up him and banged him over and over, and he was never to be seen again.

James Grisswell (10)
Shifnal Primary School, Shifnal

MY FRIEND NEMO

I met my friend Nemo at school. She was shy at first, but I got her to talk in the end. She could turn into a fish. She went into the water and that is where she got her name from. She turns into a clownfish.

One morning she asked me to come to her house so she could show me something, and of course, I said yes. After school, she pulled me up the stairs to change into a swimming costume. We went downstairs and jumped into the ocean. It was incredible.

Ava Mason (11)
Shifnal Primary School, Shifnal

THE SUPERHERO

It was day five of the battle and I was hiding behind the White House when I heard a voice. It was Dr Stupid with his robot dogs trying to find me. As quick as a flash, I flew up into the sky as I was a superhero and my name is Michael.

Oh no, I forgot Dr Stupid could fly! He chased me for ages when I heard a noise...

"Michael, wake up! You'll be late for school," my mum said... It was all just a dream. Or was it?

Miley Federico (11)
Shifnal Primary School, Shifnal

CHRISTMAS CHEER

One Christmas morning, it was jolly and bright.
Many presents under trees and kids in delight, for
outside it was snowing and the breeze was
blowing, and many children last night heard ho ho
hoing. Children were playing, playing in the snow,
wondering when the next Christmas was coming.
Delight was in the air, Christmas cheer all around
and in the jolly Christmas town, all were in the
grasp of Christmas spirit.

Grace Allatt (11)
Shifnal Primary School, Shifnal

THE DUCK AND THE BEAR

One day there was a duck. He was going on a walk. When he saw a house, the duck said, "I'll ring their doorbell."

So he went and rang the doorbell and met a bear, who was very friendly. The bear gave him some bread to eat.

"Thank you," the duck said, cheerfully. "Do you want to be friends?"

"Sure," agreed the bear. So they became the best of friends.

Megan Aston (11)

Shifnal Primary School, Shifnal

THE BLACK AND WHITE FIGURE

Swish. The door swung open in Lola's face. She tiptoed towards it. A black and white figure was running towards her. Lola was just standing still. The figure opened a black portal to the underworld. The portal was like a magnet, pulling her in suddenly. The black and white figure disappeared in the hallway and then Lola was being pulled in even more.

Kaitlyn Rowley (9)

Shifnal Primary School, Shifnal

THE BUS JOURNEY

The bus was rumbling. Fliss was chattering with her friends.

"Silence!" the teacher said. "There is a lot of traffic, so we'll be late."

The wind bashed against the bus. The wind bashed and crashed into the bus. Everybody's hearts were racing and beating, they were terrified. Every breath felt like someone punching them.

"How much longer?" said Fliss.

"Only twenty minutes left!" said the teacher.

The sun was coming down and they were looking at the different colours in the sky. The bus was squeaking.

"Oh no," said Fliss. The bus was sinking. "What's happening to us?"

Oscar Cross (10)

Tangmere Primary Academy, Tangmere

OUT OF LUCK

I stepped into the Devil's Casino, but before I could report the news, the Devil smirked, "Who goes there? Dice, is that you? You failed me thrice, I told you not to come back!"

"The-the cups are back!"

"You don't fool me, Dice! You're no match for my demons!"

I cowered behind a rock and explained seeing the cups, but the Devil responded with anger. Meanwhile, Cuphead strolled in without a care, right under the eyes of Mugman. But alas, he got hypnotised by the Casino's loot. All he needed was a lucky dice roll.

"Wish me luck," he gulped.

Dylan Brown (11)

Tangmere Primary Academy, Tangmere

THE GAME WITH MARIO!

At a big park, a girl sat playing on a Switch. Her sister called, "Lily, come and find me!"

But Lily was good at seeking. In only ten minutes she found Liv.

"It's time to go," said Lily.

"Nooo!" said Liv.

At home, in Lily's room, she still played the Super Mario game that she loved. She went downstairs into Liv's room.

"Mum wants you," said Lily.

"Okay, Lily," said Liv.

Lily ran upstairs to her room. The Switch was big; she was trapped in it. She needed to find a way out. She was being chased by Bowser!

Amelia Luff (10)

Tangmere Primary Academy, Tangmere

WW4 ENDING

"Sergeant, one shot with the missile and we have won World War Four, take the shot... Take the shot! Why are you hesitating? We're in 2094 fighting off the Congans! Take the shot!"
With that order, he loaded up the missile, put it in the rocket and prepared the shot. Three, two, o- He was hesitating to fire the missile at the poor Congans, hurt and in endless pain.
"If you don't shoot in the next ten seconds, you will be the one dying on the floor! Take the shot!"
"I have something to say..."
"Go on!"
"I am Congan!"

Theo Read (11)
Tangmere Primary Academy, Tangmere

THE NORTH POLE

One day, Santa went on a walk. He saw a little girl who had a cookie and milk. Santa went up to the little girl and said, "Hey, do you like Santa?"
The little girl said, "No, I don't like Santa."
Santa got mad and kidnapped the girl. She cried for help, but no one heard her. Santa took her to the North Pole and said, "You will become my elf for Christmas!"
The girl said, "No, I will not become your elf!"
Santa said, "Okay, but at least help me with the presents please!"
The girl said, "Okay, Santa."

Peyton Arnold-Jackman (10)
Tangmere Primary Academy, Tangmere

OH NO!

I am as scared as ever because WW3 is in its finest hour. I am an army leader for Britain and we are currently fighting for our lives. Aliens have invaded, but luckily my spine-chilling fear has gone because the hideous, just outright appalling aliens are looking like they will surrender soon! Brilliant news! Something unexpected happened. The aliens made a new weapon, but our code-breakers cracked it. I haven't written to you since February; things haven't gone to plan. I sent an email to my friend, but it got transmitted to an evil astronaut. I'm going to die...

Max Stringer (10)

Tangmere Primary Academy, Tangmere

WONDERLAND

One day in Wonderland, everybody was getting ready for the Mad Hatter's tea party, for the White Rabbit's birthday! As Alice was happily skipping, she saw a large crowd, so she went to investigate. Finally, she battled her way to the front and saw it was in the rabbit hole. She grinned and carried on her journey. When she got there and the Mad Hatter saw her, he grabbed the umbrella nearest him, screaming, "Stay back! You're crazy!"
Later that night, Alice was getting ready for bed and looked in the mirror. There was still blood on her blue dress...

Honey Clare (10)
Tangmere Primary Academy, Tangmere

ENGLAND'S WIN

It's the World Cup final between England and Germany. Germany are winning. Sterling crosses it and Kane scores. It's two-one to Germany. Gareth Southgate is making a sub. Off comes Saka, on comes a 21-year-old boy, Jack Harris.
It's the last minute, Jack Harris dribbles past three defenders, he shoots, he scores! Two-two; extra time. It's gone to penalties. Timo Werner misses one. Jack Harris to win the World Cup for England... He's done it!
England win the World Cup. Harry Kane lifts the World Cup for England. Jack Harris the hero, so, so unlikely.

Kayowa Nosiru (11)

Tangmere Primary Academy, Tangmere

SPOOKY TRIP

One dark, gloomy day, Year 6 went on a school trip. They were on their way to the woods when the engine started squeaking and slowed down. Then people started smearing their hands on the window like they were trying to get in. The hands were covered in dark red, clumpy, sticky stuff. There was something in the distance, like a shadow gliding through the horrific woods. The children were panicking and screamed while they hid under the seats.

Suddenly, everything went black. A girl woke up, drenched in sweat and realised, this whole horrific time, she was just dreaming.

Eloise Bulbeck (11)

Tangmere Primary Academy, Tangmere

BEAUTY IS A HERO

When three fairies rushed towards Aurora she asked what was wrong. They told her that tomorrow, on her sixteenth birthday, she was going to prick her finger and fall into a deep sleep, forever.

With panic, she ran towards the castle until she bumped into Prince Arthur. Once their eyes met, they fell in love. Next, Arthur told Aurora he'd help her.

After the day passed, she realised it was her birthday, so they ran until the evil fairy, Maleficent, stood in front of them. It was over. Then Aurora took Arthur's sword and struck Maleficent. Aurora was a hero.

Annabel Ridley (11)
Tangmere Primary Academy, Tangmere

WENDY'S HORROR

Wendy's heart leapt out of her chest. Finding Aster was one thing, running away from a monster was another. It was catching up. Suddenly, Wendy found something. A sword! You see, Wendy is very good at fencing. She quickly faced the intense, wild and ferocious beast, and without thinking she stabbed it.

Aster quickly hugged her. After a while, they returned to campus. Everyone ran to them, happiness filling their faces.

Loudly, the ground shook and the ceiling fell. Everyone looked up. What was it? Was the monster back again, or was it something new?

Julia Socha (11)

Tangmere Primary Academy, Tangmere

THE MERMAID TALE

One day on her ancient boat, Lola realised there was a possible crack. As quickly as possible, Lola tried to stop the water from flowing in. Finally, the water stopped.

Then, about a mile or two away, there was a mysterious island, so she decided to swim to the strange land. But she turned around and her feet had disappeared into fins. She thought she was dreaming, but she wasn't. She was a real-life mermaid!

At that moment, she didn't care about the island. Lola just wanted to swim in the crystal clear water, until she saw a small figure...

Darcy Bagnall (10)

Tangmere Primary Academy, Tangmere

A CREEPY NEIGHBOUR

One snowy day, Maddy was tucking into her supper when she spotted trucks outside her neighbour's house. Clueless, she wandered outside despite the layers of snow and realised her good friend, Sam, was not there.

Days passed but still no Sam. Maddy leapt out of her chair as the doorbell rang. An old man stood outside. He acted very nice, but one day he was watching Maddy and her family. So Maddy went to investigate.

She barely got to the front door when it swung open. The man stood there holding an axe, an evil grin spreading across his face.

Emmie Hunt (11)

Tangmere Primary Academy, Tangmere

THE MISSION

She gazed at the surface below. A sudden purple light illuminated her black shoes. They were coming. As she sprinted through the misty hallway, she eyed a vent, not too far away, and leapt onto it. She tore the door off the vent like an aggressive monkey and plunged into the safe spot. Vicious men scattered across the hallway like chess pieces, and a silhouette of a rich man walking just behind the men was spotted.

"Glad to see you," he remarked, gazing upon the decorative plant pots and rugs, before looking at the girl, desperately.

Margaret Stockdale (10)

Tangmere Primary Academy, Tangmere

THE NIGHT IN THE FOREST

It started in the gloomy night. My friends and I were playing 'it' in the forest. I was camouflaged behind an ancient log until something caught my attention. I was lost and a neon blue colour glowed in the air like the Caribbean ocean. It trailed on for around three metres. Petrified, flabbergasted, on-edge, I stumbled nearer. It looked strangely like LED lights, but it was too bright to see the actual light source. I turned to inform my friends of what I had found, then I saw a shadowy figure and heard laughter. It was just my friends.

Leo Hewitt (11)
Tangmere Primary Academy, Tangmere

THE WOODS AND THE STONE

In the woods, Jess and Jamal were lurking. They found a stone with an emerald embedded in it. They tried to pull it out as hard as they could. The stone vanished into thin air. Then it appeared a few metres away. It started chasing them as fast as they could run. They couldn't hide.

As they got closer to the edge they knew they had to jump, so they did and they landed in a cave inside the mountain. It was coming down, so they jumped again. Then they splatted all over the floor. Minutes later, they died. Oops.

Cruz Bunce (10)

Tangmere Primary Academy, Tangmere

WHAT IS IT?

Slowly, I open my eyes with my heart skipping a beat every two that fly past. Feeling the fluffy, Arctic snow fall off the edge of my numb fingertips, I stand up with a visit of fear but then look around and release my breath of worry. Red, swirly candy canes, crystal icicles letting go of a singular drop of melted water. As quick as a flash, my head whips around my body, with my feet doing a pirouette, like a ballet dancer en pointe. Footprints on the white snow behind lie like a soft duvet. What is it...?

Francessca Smith (11)
Tangmere Primary Academy, Tangmere

BACK IN TIME FOR CHRISTMAS

James was loving Christmas dinner with his family. He had left one last gift to open tonight, it was from his noxious nephew. James was about to look inside when a reality bomb set off in the middle of the present and sent them back to the dinosaur era.

James knew he had to make a time bomb, as his nephew had done this many times before at Christmas. So he had to get copper, iron, amethyst and emerald. Luckily it was easy to get. He lit it, then realised he had set the date wrong. It was too late...

Jake Burley (10)

Tangmere Primary Academy, Tangmere

MAGICAL FAIRY TALE OF UNICORNS

One sunny day, a unicorn woke up excited for a magical party. She was the happiest unicorn in her group. She was also excited for the tea party because her friends were going.

In the afternoon, at 12:20pm, the party started. She was so excited at the party, her friends were there. There was cake and sandwiches with ham and cheese. There was also tea, but then there was a magical bean from the sky. All the unicorns turned into humans and they couldn't see anything whilst the magic was happening!

Emma Walker (10)
Tangmere Primary Academy, Tangmere

THE FINAL

England vs Brazil, World Cup final. It's 3-2 to Brazil in the 88th minute. The pressure is on. Kane to Bolt, Bolt with a fabulous run. His shot missed, but Richardson has clearly taken Bolt down. It's a penalty! The little boy with the whole of England on his back. His debut relies on this world-changing penalty. He takes a few steps back, runs to the ball, shoots and he's missed.
The crowd goes silent. It's over for England. Tears fall like rain as England leave the stadium.

Frank Wright (10)
Tangmere Primary Academy, Tangmere

A DREAM IN PRISON

Carols were sung and children were ripping open presents, smiling brighter than the sun. Joy fluttered around the room like butterflies. Everyone was munching on crisp, juicy, golden turkey, which was devoured in minutes, leaving a sweet aroma around the room. Outside, the snow was falling, like it was just as happy as me. The lights were sparkling, like real fairies.

I wake up. Reality floods back to me, like a tsunami of dread. I'm in prison. I sigh and hang my head low...

Tia-Louise Keenan (10)

Tangmere Primary Academy, Tangmere

THE UNEXPECTED!

On one Tuesday morning, all the aliens were getting ready to invade the Earth! But this one particular alien, called Muck, was packing his pink, fluffy bag full of sweets.
Suddenly, his alarm for the spaceship started to buzz. Muck peacefully walked up the stairs while humming a little tune. After everyone was seated, the ship took off extremely fast. But Muck glanced over at Earth and saw an explosion go off!
Crash! The door burst open and suddenly Muck fell out!

Ami Pierce (10)

Tangmere Primary Academy, Tangmere

THE PARTY POOPER

Elena was exhausted. She had decorated the entire house in red confetti, balloons, rainbow bunting and pink and purple flowers. This was a special surprise party for her sisters, who were turning 18. Elena was nervous because her family, Uncle Ross, Auntie Ray, Mum, Dad, Gran and Ms Statale were all coming. Elena sat on her bed and started to doze off...

She stared hard around her. The room was empty! All the decorations were gone! Elena slowly realised that it was all a dream.

Ava Doherty (10)

Tangmere Primary Academy, Tangmere

IN THE WOODS

Once, in the dark, dense woods, Michael and Noah played until they bumped into Lilly. It was getting cold, so they went inside. Michael needed to go to the toilet. As he went into the toilet, he turned into a creature.

There was a loud noise, so Lilly and Noah went to go and check on him, but he was not the person they thought he was. Noah and Lilly wanted to instantly run, but Michael caught them in his giant hands... but it was all just a dream.

Amelia Miksza (11)

Tangmere Primary Academy, Tangmere

 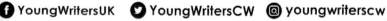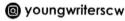